DANGEROUS UNDERCURRENTS

FBI AFFAIRS: BOOK 4

SUZANNE BAGINSKIE

Copyright © 2023 by Suzanne Baginskie

Published by DS Productions

All rights reserved.

This book may not be duplicated in any way without the express written consent of the publisher, except in the form of brief excerpts or quotations for the purposes of review.

The information contained herein is for the personal use of the reader and may not be incorporated in any commercial programs or other books, databases, or any kind of software without written consent of the publisher or author. Making copies of this book or any portion of it, for any purpose is a violation of United States copyright laws.

This is a work of fiction. Names, characters, places, and incidents either are the product of the author's imagination or are used fictitiously. Any resemblance to actual persons, living or dead, events, or locales is entirely coincidental.

ISBN: 9798854976596

❦ Created with Vellum

PROLOGUE

Miami, Florida – July, 2022

FBI Special Agent Nathan Miller glanced at his watch when the tires touched down on the Miami International runway. They'd arrived forty-five minutes late. Mumbling a curse under his breath, he blamed the industry's pilot shortage for his delayed departure. He juggled his carryon and exited the plane, blending into a busy crowd of people headed toward the baggage claim. Some of them probably had loved ones waiting at the other end. Fifty-five and single, he'd never married. No significant other would be there to greet him.

Miller's thoughts focused on his prior week vacation spent on Cancun's sandy beach, where he'd relaxed beneath the hot Mexican sun, cooled off in the Caribbean Sea, and downed too many margaritas. Last night, he'd enjoyed drinks in a tiki hut bar with an attractive female.

She sat on the stool next to him and shared her tale of woe. Her fourteen-year-old sister never came home after a night spent partying on that very same beach. Two years had passed and still no news of her whereabouts.

Squinting at her, he listened intently, and never uttered a word about his FBI status at the Cybercrime, Human Trafficking and Homicide Division back in the states. He'd heard this same sad story repeated many times before and came on this trip to definitely unwind. Eight months from now, he'd submit his twenty-year retirement date and then sit back and collect his pension and do more of the same. He finished his drink, placed the empty glass on the counter and asked for a refill.

An hour later and after a few more margaritas, they toasted the scenic Mexican sunset as it disappeared into the turquoise ocean. She rose and asked, "Would you like to have a nightcap in my hotel room?" He grinned and couldn't refuse. Memories of their last night together warmed his loins.

Until reality sank in. Had his reserved ride stuck around? He pulled his iPhone from his pants pocket and speed dialed. The reservation had been made under the fictitious name of *Jackson*, which most likely rose across the man's cell screen. The driver answered on the first ring.

"This is Luis, Mr. Jackson. I know your flight was delayed. The good news is I'm close by. See you in about twenty?"

"Sounds good." Miller tucked his phone away and spotted his suitcase revolving along the curved carousel tract headed in his direction. He reached down, yanked the bag into an upright position, and wheeled it toward the outdoor pickup area. Confident no one would recognize him, he maneuvered through the crowd dressed like a tourist in tan cargo shorts, tropical shirt, and sunglasses. When he paused at the curb, he blended in among dozens of people on the sidewalk searching the road for their ride. Voices buzzed around him, and the high humidity formed beads of perspiration that threatened to drip on his brow. He sighed and inhaled, deeply breathing in a mixture of bus, automobile, and taxicab exhaust fumes. He covered his mouth and coughed. Welcome back to the city of Miami.

Miller scanned the roadway. Where was his driver? He glanced at his wristwatch; more than twenty minutes had passed. Should he call for another? A splash of red stopped beside him. He turned. Idling at the curb sat a red Honda Civic, its magnetic business sign hung on the door. The driver lowered the passenger window and asked, "Are you Mr. Jackson?"

Agent Miller nodded.

"I'm Luis."

Miller steered his luggage to the rear end of the vehicle.

The guy hopped out, hurried to his trunk, and tossed Miller's carryon bag and suitcase inside. "Please be seated in the back, sir."

Miller climbed in.

Thin, maybe five foot eight with thick curly hair, Luis slid in behind the steering wheel. His coffee-brown eyes peered at Miller through the rearview mirror. "Where to exactly?"

Miller replied with an address two blocks from the FBI complex where he'd left his car parked. Protecting his true identity had become quite necessary in the last few years. Working in Miami at the FBI for almost ten years, he lived in the north section of town. Not a long trip, except on Sunday mornings when devout church goers left their homes for worship and increased the stream of cars.

Rush-hour traffic couldn't have been worse. Once they reached Interstate 75, the three car lanes moved forward at the speed of snails. Luis cursed under his breath; he headed for the exit lane and tailgated behind a few others. On the main highway, he made a left.

It should have been right. "Wait, you're headed south. I live in north Miami. Make a U-turn up ahead," Miller said.

Luis smiled wide, and merely shrugged. His smartphone

rang, saving him from a response. He tapped the speaker button and an accented male voice spoke. "Luis, where are you?" Luis named the highway. He glanced in the rearview and met Miller's eyes. "My passenger's flight was delayed." He paused. "Tell them I'll pick them up soon."

Miller's relaxing week vacation had helped him release some of his pent-up anxiety. Was he overthinking again? Miles from his condo, he questioned the route the guy had taken. He shut his eyes, drew in a deeper breath, and kept himself from jumping to conclusions. When his driver finally made a right-hand turn, Miller figured the guy realized he'd headed in the wrong direction.

Miller gazed out the window as Luis passed a few opportunities to head farther north. He never slowed. He continued on a narrow roadway; nothing but vegetation lined either side, until they reached an old wooden barn fronting a deserted orange grove. Luis eased the vehicle over the rocky paved driveway. He stopped, cut the engine, and unsnapped his seatbelt.

"What's going on?" Miller asked. He patted his shoulder area where the holster he always wore should have been. Nothing. An automatic reflex. Traveling on an airplane from the U.S. into Mexico and back, weapons weren't allowed.

Luis reached below, pulled the hood release lever. It jerked open. He climbed out, slammed the driver's door, and the locks clicked in unison.

Agent Miller unfastened his seatbelt and wiggled his passenger door handle. It wouldn't budge. Adrenalin coursed through him. "Unlock this door!" He banged his knuckles hard against the glass window, twice, and glared at Luis as he walked by. A smirk slithered over his thin lips, as he ignored him and disappeared behind the vehicle.

Miller watched the rear trunk raise, and then Luis slammed it shut. He carried a red gas can and paced forward as if on a mission. If they were out of gas, the tank should be on the driver's side. Through the windshield, he watched Luis lift the car's hood and then moved side to side. Had he splashed gasoline over the entire engine?

Miller's heart thudded in his chest. The familiar odor seeped through the car's vents and went straight into his nostrils. "Wait." He struggled to catch his breath as he hurled himself over the front seat and hit the main unlock button. The doors wouldn't budge. He choked out, "You have to get me out of here. Unlock these doors."

Luis produced a lighter from his top pocket.

Miller's face twisted in horror.

Luis flicked the lighter. The flame came alive, flickering in the slight breeze.

Miller banged his knuckles harder this time. "No. Wait. Luis, I'll pay you double...even more than whoever arranged this." His voice cracked as he yelled through the interior glass. "Name your price?" Seconds ticked away. He waited for an answer. None came. He lay back flat, kicked both feet at the car's side window several times. It wouldn't break. He opened the glove box. Totally empty. Not a tool inside to help him. He scrambled over the front seats and back to the rear compartment. His shaking hands clawed at the back seat, again and again. It wouldn't loosen. He cursed and pounded on the side window once more.

In his peripheral vision, he noticed Luis's wicked grin as he tossed the lighter into the engine and closed the hood. He saw the flames glow orangish-red through the vent openings.

An old Ford truck's muffler roared as it drove across the stony path. The driver stomped on the brakes and Luis sprinted over and leaped inside.

Miller grabbed his cell phone. His thumbs twitched as he dialed nine-one-one. He pressed the phone to his ear as the vehicle drove from sight. Rampant thoughts invaded his head. In the past, perps he'd forcefully put into jail had threatened to kill him. Trapped, without a chance of an escape, he figured one had actually outsmarted him. They'd planned a way to get even. A nine-one-one operator answered, "How can I help you?"

The last thing he heard was an explosion.

1

Miami, Florida
FBI Administration Building

Monday morning, FBI Special Agent Elaine Bishop guided her official vehicle inside the covered garage and pulled into her designated spot. Working daily at the imposing building, she weaved through the maze of security checkpoints and smiled at workers she passed by often. FBI Headquarters pulsed as usual. Highly trained operatives monitored the network twenty-four-seven. Their surveillance and scanning devices grew more sophisticated each day. She strolled toward her office in the Cybercrime, Human Trafficking, and Homicide division, her thoughts concentrated on their most active drug case.

By the time she entered the cubical and sat in her swivel chair, she'd visualized an alternative plan for the team to avoid an ill-fated mission at all costs. She loved solving puzzles and breaking codes and had an intuitive knack for spotting patterns while others could not. Fresh in her mind, she jotted the essential specifics on a legal pad. Glancing over at the July calendar, she frowned. With August approaching next week, several updated report deadlines would be due this Friday. Her outlined proposal would remain on hold. She sighed, tapped her keyboard and a familiar ping sounded. After inserting her memorized password, she waited as assorted icons populated her screen.

An urgent memo from Director Croft materialized over them.

Tension bubbled inside her. The Director didn't contact agents unless something huge had happened. Without another thought, she clicked opened the email. The further she read, the more her heart rate increased. Tears threatened. She inhaled deeply, even looked away for a few seconds, but the words remained unchanged. She reread the first paragraph again.

"I'm sorry to report that a body we believe to be FBI Special Agent Nathan Miller was discovered earlier this morning in a vehicle severely damaged by a fiery explosion at an old Miami orange grove. Dental records will certify his identity. Evidence found at the scene helped corroborate the individual's remains. Authorities believe his death may not be accidental, and stated he could have been targeted."

Tears stung her eyes clogging her vision. They trickled lower dampening her cheeks, she grabbed a tissue and swiped. Her eyesight blurry, she blinked clearing it and then refocused on the memo. She glanced over at Miller's empty chair. Gone on a much needed week vacation, he flew into Miami Sunday afternoon, but according to the memo, he never arrived home. Someone had murdered him. Why? With all his years of experience, how had this happened?

As her ranking division leader, she'd worked with him for the last five years. Bishop had been assigned to his unit straight out of Quantico. Before long, she proved she could hold her own. Agent Miller recognized her value at planned stakeouts, she was at the top of her game, sharp and physically strong. Fierce confidence helped her achieve special agent status, sooner than a few of her male counterparts. Their compatibility made them inseparable and outside of work, and they enjoyed a close friendship. After her parents died in a car accident three years ago only her younger brother, Jessie, had survived. Miller watched over her like a father figure. Reading this memo about his loss, triggered powerful images that morphed into more grief, and shattered what she hoped would have become a long friendship.

A rap sounded on the doorframe. Weber, her other partner. He always announced his arrival with a knock. It usually made her laugh. Today, it wasn't funny.

She blew her nose and dabbed another tissue at her face. Her fingers smoothed her shoulder-length, highlighted brunette hair. As a professional dressed in a black suit and comfortable flats, she arrived eager and ready for business until Director Crofton's email spread across her screen and mentally shook her. Biting her bottom lip, she fought the urge to panic and tried hard to control her emotions. The bearer of sad news, she was about to ruin his day, too.

In walked FBI Special Agent Weber. "Good morning, Bishop." He stood there looking confident and composed, a briefcase tightly clutched in his right hand. His face clean-shaven, and brown hair neatly trimmed, he'd worn a well-cut navy blue suit, and acted ready to face another week.

She focused on eye contact, something her Quantico psyche trainer had taught to personalize her interactions and keep her mind concentrating. "Good morning, Weber. I'm glad you're here." After her assessing gaze, she continued. "An important message from Director Croft has arrived."

His smile faded, and his hazel-green eyes narrowed. "What's happened now?"

"I hate to tell you this, but earlier this morning, they found Agent Miller dead. Killed in a fiery car explosion." She rose, walked toward him crushing back her own disbelief, not readily accepting the horrible truth of her own words, and not the way to start their Monday morning.

"No...I don't believe it." Weber flinched and dropped his case. It thudded on the floor. He moved closer. "I had a text from him on Saturday. Are they certain?"

"Almost. I only know what was written in the director's memo. The explosion hurled pieces of the car into in the open field. They found the remains of a suitcase and a small fireproof document box. It contained Miller's gold badge, ID, and a couple of passports All his other belongings were destroyed."

Agent Weber stepped closer and gently slid his arms around her. She felt herself go limp in his embrace and wept on his shoulder. They lingered in silence for a short while. When they parted, she stepped back and turned toward her desk, trembling. In the three years since he was hired, they'd never been that close to each other before. She'd never experienced his warmth or inhaled his cologne. All the time the three of them spent working together as a team, she didn't want to believe one of her trusted co-workers had suddenly lost his life and so horribly.

She glanced at Weber. "Croft did mention Miller's return flight had been delayed forty-five minutes. No other vehicles were present in the orange grove, so it wasn't a normal car accident." She shook her head. "Croft's memo also stated Miller may have been targeted."

She'd experienced harsh words spoken from an inmate or two in the past, as had other FBI special agents attending their perp's final sentencing hearing. Most of them joked about it as the bailiff dragged them from the courtroom. Ninety-nine out of a hundred inmates threats never came to fruition. Unless one perp with long arms reaching outside of prison, put a hit out on Miller.

"This is such a shock. His Chevy Suburban's parked in the FBI garage, I really thought he beat me in this morning." His stared at the floor and remained silent for a few seconds. "Miller always used a transport service when he traveled back and forth to the airport. Have they contacted them? Do they know who the vehicle was registered too?"

"Nothing yet from the local police." A thousand questions cluttered her mind. "They're waiting for us at the scene."

"Hang in there. I'm so sorry to hear the news. It sure won't be the same around here without him." He hesitated, "This is just terrible, but we'll get whoever's responsible for Miller's death. It's only a matter of time. He grabbed his briefcase. "I'll put this in my office, and we'll rush over there." He gazed at her. "Bishop are you okay? I bet we both could use some caffeine. Let's go fill our thermos with coffee before we leave."

"Nothing will help at this point, but that's a good idea." She sighed and picked up their empty containers.

"We'll find out who did this Bishop. If it's the last thing we ever do, I promise."

She nodded and trailed him through the doorway. He reached the break room first and shoved the door open. She entered into the room's familiar scent of coffee and hurried to the counter. Tears splashed from her lashes as she filled their two travel cups, she'd need more time to process his loss.

"I wondered if the morning news knows about this?" He aimed the remote at a television set mounted in the corner on a steel frame.

"This just in." Hearing the male newscaster's voice, she turned. "Police have found an unidentified man's body burned to death inside a vehicle at a deserted orange grove on the outskirts of Miami."

His words thundered in her ears. She clenched the thermos tighter and watch the flashing images on the screen. A reporter's camera focused on an old barn with a barren orange grove behind it. It swayed slowly sideways and concentrated on three parked police cars. Their red and blue lightbars revolved on the screen. The next shot featured what was left of the vehicle's burnt frame. She muffled a sob.

He continued, "The nine-one-one caller first reported they saw a mannequin on fire in the old field. Turned out they were wrong. It was human."

Reality hit her like a death sentence for a second time. Her stomach rumbled and adrenaline coursed through her veins. With her closest confidant gone, how would she carry on? She wouldn't be able to sleep until they arrested the perp and stuck him behind bars. Tightening the thermos cap, she glanced over at agent Weber. They all worked together so well in their unit. She always had their back and they hers. With Miller gone, who would fill in that gap?

Weber swerved her way. "What about his informant, maybe it was him?"

"Don't even go there. I want this person caught as much as you do, but…"

"He's the most likely candidate. He could be double crossing us and playing both sides. How can we even trust him?"

She searched his face. "That's to be determined. He's risked a lot to keep Miller informed."

"Well, he hasn't checked in for over a week. Maybe he got spooked and spilled the beans." Weber pressed the TV's off button, seized his cup and headed toward the door.

"Then he'd lose the witness protection he so dearly wanted

for his wife and their two-year-old daughter. Consider that." She glared at him.

"His so called pals are smart. What makes you think they didn't catch on to him? Especially hearing this news. Who knows, they might be responsible for Miller's death. When we return, I'll go over Miller's file and see where he left off. Then, I'll set a meeting with his snitch." Weber pried open the door.

"Sound good. For now, we better get going." They approached the cubicles that linked them all closely together. Each one identically furnished on the agency's small budget. Three desktop computers, wooden desks, and rolling chairs with a copier and file cabinet to share. Not one of their offices offered much privacy. From today on, Miller's office would sit empty. Not by choice, and minus one very seasoned worker. Bishop grabbed her purse, knowing down deep inside her without his guidance, their division would never be the same.

WEBER USHERED Bishop through the building's security surveillance system, and into the parking garage. The sight of Miller's parked black van kindled anger inside him. He gritted his teeth, looked away and tapped his Suburban's key fob. When the doors beeped open, they both hurried inside. He followed the worn red exit signs that needed replacing toward the exit. Bishop held their ID's and gold badges in her lap ready to present them for the security guard's approval.

He drove through the dim lighting of the FBI garage and straight out into the bright morning sun. Slipping on his Ray Bans, he joined the stream of idling vehicles awaiting their turn at the security booth. Once they were vetted, the guard pressed a release button and the metal gate swung apart. Weber eased on the gas pedal and soon blended into heavy traffic on the busy Miami city streets.

Bishop sat quiet, her expression flat. He'd worked with her for the last three years and suspected she was trying to be brave. Always preoccupied with agent Miller, she fussed over him more than she let on. She'd most likely taken his loss quite badly. When he first arrived this morning, he'd noticed immediately her stormy green eyes narrowed with concern. Smart and sensitive, she always used her intellect in an untenable situation. She evaluated everything and relied on her instincts. Working with her, he respected her fears and her gutsy decisions. For some unknown reason, she'd kept a cool relationship with him. But when Weber hugged her earlier, he felt the magnetic pull between them. Where did that come from? She smelled like roses and fit right into his arms. Right now, he knew she'd need someone. He'd be there for her if she let him.

He'd promised himself not to get involved with another woman after his last girlfriend broke his heart. She turned him against romance, forever. He pushed those thoughts away knowing Bishop would surely need his support. His heart ached for Miller, too. Deep down inside him, he would need hers.

He sped down the highway, changed lanes and headed south out of town. The closer they came, the more his mind crowded with unanswered questions. Reality set in. What happened to Miller could happen to him. He dreaded viewing the crime scene. Not a pleasant situation for either of them. Somehow, he'd face the awful truth his longtime partner had been horribly murdered. He hoped this last look would finalize Miller's death.

Agent Weber drove his Suburban onto the stony pavement and parked aside an old barn as had other official vehicles. Red paint peeled off the barn like an apple's outer layer of skin, exposing the weathered wood beneath. Off the beaten track, the place sure didn't resemble the inner city of Miami where the high-rise office buildings accented the scenery.

Weber walked toward the scene breathing in remnants of smoke-filled fumes. The deserted land once housed a healthy orange grove. Instead of colorful oranges dangling from the straggly branches, Spanish moss filled in the void. Sadly, a section of scorched marks on the weedy grass had been cordoned off by yellow crime scene tape. Behind it, rows of neglected trees marked for death stood in the unkempt grove. Thank goodness the fire hadn't spread further. Once robust and high producing, their drooping branches would have succumbed to the flames.

Uniformed officers guarded the enclosed area fending off a couple of pesky reporters and their cameraman ready to film. Nothing got passed the press. They used social media, Facebook, and Twitter. At times they knew about the crime scene before the local police. He wondered if they spied on the nine-one-one calls.

A local paramedics van sat next to three black and white police cars haphazardly parked on the sidelines. Two uniformed medics and five or so officers stood huddled together sipping coffee and in deep conversation. Firefighters dressed in full gear struggled with rewinding a lengthy hose around a large wheel on the shiny lime-yellow fire truck.

Weber only arrived moments ago, and Florida's intense temperatures and humidity had already caused him to sweat beneath his jacket. He wiped his forehead and studied the burnt steel automobile frame resting in its own ashes. His stomach turned. No one could have survived that explosion! Broken shards of glass windows were scattered everywhere. High heat from the fire melted the rubber tires right off the metal spokes that were still attached to the sway bars. Fragments of steel littered the ground like shrapnel. The flames had licked at whatever waited in its path.

"Bishop lets headed toward that taller man wearing a tie and two-piece black suit. He's probably the lead detective."

"I'll follow you."

Traveling across the field, Weber's shoes crunched on dirt, and strands of brittle grass clung to his suit pants. Tension coiled in his muscles. He ignored it.

The man turned when they approached.

"I'm FBI Special Agent Weber, and this is my partner, Special Agent Bishop. He pried his ID and gold badge from his jacket pocket and presented them. Are you in charge here?"

"I am. Detective Murray's my name." Sweat dotted his brow. He pulled out a handkerchief and mopped his forehead.

"The bureau sent us here because one of your officers phoned in a violent homicide death. FBI will now officially handle this case." Weber braced for the usual backlash he'd received from prior experiences. Whenever the FBI trumped these local guys, they weren't always happy about the intrusion.

Murray smirked and veered toward his officers. "Boys, our services are no longer required here. Please cooperate and give these agents any information and evidence you've found."

"What have you got so far?" Agent Weber asked.

"Follow me." Murray ducked beneath the yellow tape and stepped inside the marked off crime zone. An awful smell of gasoline mixed with smoldered metal hung thick in the air. He nodded at his forensic tech who moved closer to the blue tarp.

Bishop handed Weber a set of black rubber gloves and slipped her fingers into another pair. Weber elevated the yellow tape high enough so Bishop could pass, then he ducked and followed her inside the damaged area. He removed his sunglasses, stuck on the latex gloves, and the tech lifted the cover.

Weber gasped when he saw the victim. Only a blackened corpse remained. He'd never seen worse. The flesh and skin were entirely charred off, not one bit of facial structure remained. Body parts had been burned beyond recognition. Blacker than coal, the form laying there didn't resemble anything human. His gaze landed on Bishop. Color had drained from her flawless face, and she quickly turned away.

"Do you know the exact cause of death? Any bullet holes?" Weber asked and studied the victim again. For some unknown reason, the killer didn't want anyone to identify the body. He wondered why?

"No, we have nothing. Our coroner ruled the death as Immolation caused by the extreme blaze and explosion that most likely smothered him and singed off his skin. No gunshot wounds anywhere, and no extremities have been removed. He determined the body was male. We found him lying right here near the rear of what's left of the vehicle's chassis."

"Who originally called this in?" Weber eyes searched Murray's face. Deep black circles bordered his brownish eyes from lack of sleep. He probably arrived in the wee hours of the morning and already consumed too much caffeine.

"An anonymous caller. He used a burner phone and must have destroyed the Sim card. Too short a call for my deputy to trace. We rushed right over and located the body, or the poor soul would still be lying here alone." He glanced around and then sighed.

"Any estimate on the time of death?" Weber shifted his stance.

"The coroner said he hoped to determine that later at the lab." He stared directly into Weber's eyes. "If there's enough of him to work with." Murray swerved sideways. "Larry, bring over all the evidence your guys discovered in the grove."

A stout man nodded and dashed toward one of the black

and white patrol cars. He reached inside the trunk and lifted out a large plastic bag. He ventured over. "Here's what they found so far. We believe it's what's left of the contents in a burnt suitcase. They found a fireproof document box untouched by the flames still inside. It held passports and a federal gold badge. That's how we knew to contact the bureau."

"Have you dusted that for prints? Or walked the area grid?" Bishop asked.

"Yes and no. Not all of it. I'll send you the print info later, but as far as the grid, the case is now yours. Be my guest." Murray paused. "We've only examined this section where the crime tape is installed. When we arrived, this was the only vehicle at the scene. Tire tracks over there proved another automobile, probably the get-away car had recently been here. Looks like they pealed out. Your forensic team can take prints." He pointed to the section of land closer to the road. "Over there, we found the car's license plate. The blast must have blown it off, but it didn't burn too badly, and is still readable. An officer saw it lying in the weeds and ran the number. Of course, it came back reported as stolen."

"That sure figures, don't it." Weber shook his head. He knew the local police department would only help the FBI so much. Not unusual, that's how they worked. He looked at Bishop. "Please call our Rookies. Get them here to help walk the grid. Also, ask them to contact the forensic tech team and our medical examiner." She nodded and walk toward their SUV.

Murray checked his watch and seemed eager to depart. "If you don't have any more questions for us, I'll let my men go home."

"That's fine. Thanks for all your help. Please remember to forward that recording of the anonymous phone call to my office."

"Will do. Take care, Weber." He turned on his boot heels and headed toward his men.

Bishop strolled over, her face had grief written all over it. "Forensics and a couple of rookies are on the way. They're contacting the coroner. I'll take some photos of the corpse and the remains of the car for our files. I guess they didn't find any weapons on the scene?"

"Nope, Miller couldn't fly to Mexico with any. I just hope he had a great vacation before all this. Poor guy, he didn't deserve to die this way." His words echoed in his own ears. He'd never seen a murdered victim quite like this.

"I agree. It's a horrible death for sure. Someone will pay dearly." She stood on her toes.

As if in deep thought, he saw her stare into the distance and then lower her sunglasses.

"I see something reddish beneath those trees." She pointed. "I'll check it out."

He watched her hike the grove and weave in and out of several rows of dead orange trees.

Ten minutes later she returned. "Weber. There's a red gas can over there. It reeks of gasoline. I'm sure someone used it to start the fire. The killer must have tossed it into the field. Let's hope his prints are on it. I took more pictures and will notify forensics when they arrive. It could be a useful source of evidence." She smiled.

"You have good eyes, Bishop and we didn't start walking the grid yet. It might be best piece of evidence we have so far." He studied her face. As she spoke of her discovery, a smile rose on her lips lighting up her features. Her green eyes sparkled at him. He'd never noticed her smile before or had he ever really looked? Working alongside her, he'd always treated her like one of the guys.

He'd sworn off the dating scene years ago and never hung

out at the clubs. He enjoyed his own company at home watching crime shows and drinking Tito's vodka. The memory of his fiancé tossing her engagement ring in his face still hurt. After he'd courted her for two years, she ran off with another guy. Brokenhearted, he vowed never to let another woman in. Period and so far, it had worked out fine. Now at age thirty-five, his FBI assignments filled his days and nights and that's how he liked it.

AGENT BISHOP SQUATTED beside Agent Miller's covered remains scrutinizing the whole scene. They'd been there over an hour, and she hadn't seen one car drive by. This deserted part of town had no bars, restaurants, or office buildings. The area appeared abandoned for a couple of miles each way. It made a perfect place to kill someone. She rose and breathed deeply, calming herself.

Had he been awake or unconscious before the explosion? The whole incident sounded brutal. She couldn't understand why anyone could be this cruel. No way she could stop thinking about Miller's murder. She concluded it had to be premeditated. She couldn't find any sign of a struggle or even a drop of blood for DNA testing. She forced herself to concentrate. Numbness penetrated deep inside her soul, and her heart ached really bad.

She swallowed hard, uncovered his body, and visually examined it again. She needed to document the scene. This time she frowned. All the usual signs of death were missing like flies! Not one fly or any putrid smell of death and no sign of decay. Was this an execution-like murder committed in an odd way? The questions she needed answered would go unasked, without any witnesses.

Why did this happen to Miller? Who would benefit from it? His informant? Maybe the head gang leader ordered his C.I. to take him out? Had the snitch lied to save himself? Drug traffickers and their prostitute business ran rampant in Miami and were not easy to bust. She had no answers and many situations to consider, with none of the usual clues. Someone wanted him out of the way bad enough to end his life. Period. This investigation would take more than one day. She draped the blue tarp over him gently.

His loss made her feel helpless. He'd been her rock since her parents died in a car accident. Her fifteen-year-old brother, Jessie, was a passenger in the back seat. He ended up in a two month coma. Currently, Jessie resided at a center for brain injured patients. She hadn't seen him in over two weeks. Not that he would remember, he didn't even recognize her. The doctor said his memory could return at any time. Three years later, and it never happened. She shut her eyes for a few seconds. Guilt teetered in her mind. "This too shall pass," she whispered and reopened them.

At nearly noon, the high July sun caused perspiration on her brow. She avoided looking where the body lay and wiped away her sweat. Behind her a vehicle's tires crunched against the stone drive. She turned and saw a black SUV parking. The rookies had arrived, followed by the coroner, and their crime scene techs.

The medical examiner carried his black bag and hiked over to where she stood. Tall with a shiny bald head, he wore a white shirt, blue tie, and navy slacks. They exchanged greetings. He encased his fingers inside plastic gloves and ducked beneath the yellow ribbon. When he lifted the tarp and viewed the corpse, she saw him shake his head. "What a horrible way to die."

"Especially for FBI Special Agent Miller."

"I agree. No clues on who, what or why, I guess?"

"Nothing yet."

He frowned. "I'll have to do some calculations, factor in the combustion, exposure to extreme heat and hot gases before I can determine a time of death."

"Sounds complicated for sure. We haven't much to go on, except for the fireproof box with his badge and passports." She hoped he didn't notice the despair in her voice.

"Dental records should definitely confirm if it's him. I'm so sorry for his loss. A good man. One of the best at the bureau. He will be sorely missed." He motioned to the paramedics waiting on the sidelines. "Bishop, I will have to move his body to the morgue for further examination. I can't do anything else here."

Bishop nodded. "I completely understand. I figured your exam will be as bewildering as ours." She took one last look at Miller's body and promised herself to stop at nothing until she found his killer.

Ten feet away, Weber stood scribbling notes on his pad. She approached him. Over six foot tall, she had to look up at him from her five foot six height. "What are you thinking?"

"I'm recording this as an execution style murder, one that robs of us from all the clues necessary to track the people responsible."

"I totally agree. A well planned murder and thought out down to the get-away car. We should try to locate neighbors in this area, but I don't think there are too many living here that could identify anyone. Unless they saw a car frequently traveling by and casing the grove."

"You may have something there. I'll have one of the rookies drive a couple of miles in both directions and canvass the close neighborhood." Weber stuck his pad in his pocket.

"Miller probably thought the transport driver came from his usual company. Which means somebody knew he'd be returning from that trip and that his plane was late. They canceled his other driver and made a switch. Money talks. They pulled off an elaborate plan to take him down." Bishop tightened her lips.

Weber nodded. "The Rookies are already walking the grid. I told them about that gas can. So far, they haven't discovered anything else. We should return to headquarters and start checking out his current files."

"Can we stop somewhere for a cold drink? I'm done with the hot coffee."

"I agree. Follow me to the Suburban and I'll see if we can find a lunch place farther into town."

"I'm not sure I can eat. My stomach's churning. But a really cold iced tea and a bathroom would be great."

"Understandable. I'll second that."

Twenty-five minutes later, they sat in the back corner of a burger place drinking iced tea and sharing a chicken sandwich. "This is refreshing and clever idea on the sandwich. The air conditioning in this place feels great. In fact, I am almost too cold." She smiled at him.

Two twenty-something guys with black-inked tattoos on their biceps came in arguing.

Weber frowned and put down his iced tea.

The men simmered some when the clerk asked for their order.

Bishop saw Weber's shoulders relax. The agency taught it's agents to be watchful at all times. Maybe he thought they wanted to rob the place. It happened a lot more in today's world.

They walked by carrying their food trays, arguing about football teams and the winner of the next weekend's game.

He shook his head. "We have enough problems, sorry for ignoring you when those guys came in."

"I understand, you don't have to apologize. We're FBI. We live on the edge with our sixth sense for trouble."

"You got that right. Alertness is one of my vices and I stay prepared at all times. When you're finished, let's go back to the office and I'll do a background check on the transportation company Miller used. It's a start. I'll also contact the airport and ask them to forward their security film of the pickup area."

She trailed behind him as he carried their trays to the trash bin. After he disposed of their garbage, Weber headed for the door and opened it. His manners were impeccable. The two men watched their every move as they had theirs. Maybe dressed in business suits, they stood out in the fast food place.

2

Weber slouched behind his desk. He phoned the airport transportation company Miller regularly used for his flights. They confirmed there was no record of a scheduled return trip. Weber searched for a list of other transport places that serviced Miami International. He hoped by contacting them, one would have Miller's name registered on their pickup list. The film he'd ordered from the pickup area may have captured the company's vehicle and the driver's face. At this point, they had nothing else to go on.

He glanced over at Bishop's cubicle. The small glass partitions between them didn't serve their privacy well. As if frozen in place, her focus remained on the monitor. Bishop disagreed with him on how to investigate Miller's death. She preferred working in minute details and sequence and spent her time rereading from page one on her computer. Miller's latest notes merited his attention, first.

When Weber joined their unit three years ago, it didn't take him long to notice agent Bishop favored Miller over him. He got the impression she leaned on the guy almost like a father figure. Weber worked with other female agents in his past, and on several undercover missions. Compared to them, Bishop showed the greatest courage and field experience of any FBI woman he ever partnered with. This afternoon he saw a different side of her. He'd noticed her emerald-green eyes were bloodshot, and her usual zing had disappeared.

Their three person team solved various dangerous crimes together for the last couple of years. One event stood out more than the rest, when the gangs in Miami were one step ahead of them selling fentanyl to younger kids at an elementary school. Agent Bishop's close investigation undermined a fourth grader selling his wares to third grade students. She befriended him as a dealer, he purchased drugs from her, and she praised his bravery and business success at such a youthful age. Immature, he fell for it, hook, line, and sinker. His victims, nine-year-old school children, thought they were buying expensive candy. She arrested him and took him to a juvenile detention center before anyone else died. The thought still sickened Weber. Drug problems existed in many of the states, but Florida's accessible coastline had more than their fair share.

Shocked through and through, he'd never have thought they be investigating a homicide for one of their own, their ranking leader, Miller.

Agent Bishop glanced over from her cubicle. "Weber, we should go downtown right now and locate Miller's snitch and bring him in for questioning."

"I want this head guy as much as you Bishop, but that would expose our hand to those traffickers. They'd be on to us in a minute. We need to lay low for a while on this case." He sucked in a deep breath. "Miller risked a lot to serve up these perps and if their leader, Santiago gets a whiff their guy, Richie Cruz is in cahoots with the FBI, him, his wife and daughter will all end up dead."

"Maybe not, if we play our hand right." She pursed her lips.

"We can get them into the witness protection plan as soon as Cruz provides the goods."

"What if he doesn't, they'll kill them anyway for squealing. If they arranged Miller's death, then we know for sure his informant's life's in danger. These people are not trustworthy. He hasn't checked in since last week because Miller told him he'd be out of town."

"Agent Weber?" A female voice spoke through the intercom system.

"Yes. What's up, Jen?"

"Agent Johnson's holding on line three. Says it's real important and to put you right through."

"Thanks." He grabbed the receiver. "Agent Weber."

"Johnson, here. This will be short, but not sweet. We found another body. Called in by a clerk at the King Convenience store off exit 7A of Interstate 75. I'm here now. I think you and Bishop should come right over. The victim's a male. He's partially burned because someone threw him inside a dumpster at the rear of their store."

"Whoa. Thanks for the call. We'll see you soon."

FIFTEEN MINUTES LATER, Weber and Bishop approached the crime scene and darted into the King Convenience store's parking lot. Pedestrians clogged the sidewalk, horns honked, sirens rang out and air brakes hissed on passing trucks. Two policemen had cordoned off the area and worked hard to keep the noisy crowd under control.

An older neighborhood, they hiked around the twenty-year old structure inhaling the lingering acrid scent. Behind the building sat a lime-yellow fire truck and paramedic's van. Bishop stopped short when they neared the steel dumpster, large puddles had pooled around the unit. Firefighters had sprayed gallons of water battling the blaze. They also soaked the store's roof and dampened it's exterior store walls; cooling down the building to prevent further damage. The outdoor fire didn't signal the internal water sprinklers. Good news for the owners, all their merchandise and employees had been spared. As soon as the fire chief discovered the body in the dumpster, he ruled out arson; and followed their procedure to preserve the initial evidence.

Bishop's eyes paused on the white tarp covering the body, brown shoes stuck out one end. No matter how many times she'd seen a corpse, her emotions ran high. Today brought two unexpected fatalities. Both lives were taken by fire. This one still resembled a human form, but oh the pain he must have endured. She forced herself to separate her immediate sadness so she could do her job. As an FBI agent, she needed to focus on the matter at hand as her Quantico instructor had taught. For her this was one of the hardest tasks to accomplish, beside killing a person.

Yellow crime scene tape waved at them in the sight breeze. Would this murder be linked to the other? Today, unexpectedly brought two deaths by fire, which was one of the most difficult crime scene investigations to solve. Weber stood alongside the deceased. She inhaled the awful smell of garbage as she approached him. Agent Johnson uncovered the victim. The unknown man lay flat on his back, his burnt arms exposed, and his hair singed. He had second and third degree burn's all over his body. Dressed in somewhat torn dungarees, and what use to be a black t-shirt, it appeared the kill had been intentional. His reddish face suffered bad burns, hopefully fingerprints remained for identification.

"Lucky for us, someone noticed flames coming from the dumpster and called nine-one-one and then told the store owner," Johnson said. "When they fished this guy out of there, his wallet fell from his pocket pretty much intact. We've found a driver's license."

"Is the man who reported the fire still here? Maybe he saw more than he's telling." Weber asked.

"We have his information, but he had to get back to work. Said he didn't see anything but the flames. He figured someone tossed a lit cigarette inside. Happens a lot."

"What the victim's name?" Bishop couldn't wait any longer.

"His license says Ritchie Cruz."

"She gasped and turned to Weber. "That Miller's informant."

His face paled. He grabbed his phone and dialed. "Jen, it's Weber. Please connect me with Agent Perez as fast as possible." He covered one ear as traffic passed by and walked toward the building.

Bishop knew Cruz's wife and child needed immediate protection and should be whisked out of town. Agent Perez specialized in their WitSec program. In less than a day, his wife and child would be in the Witness Protection System somewhere far away from here. They'd start a new life without her husband. Her tears would flow, but in time she'd realize how much safer they were. The gang must have figured out her husband played them as an informant. So, they killed Agent Miller first and then him. Bishop knew those who played with fire lived by fire, and the gang's lethal life of crime had no regard for family. Anyone who stood in their way would be eliminated.

The medical examiner's van arrived. He rushed over. "I never thought I'd see you both again on the same day."

"Neither did we." Bishop backed up to allow him a closer view.

The crime scene techs wore Tyvek suits and went to work fencing off the area and placing their numerical markers. She watched the coroner kneel by his second victim. He turned him on his stomach. "There's indication of strangulation marks around his throat area, but he may have only blacked out. It's obvious his death resulted from the intense heat and combustion."

"They probably used the arson to help cover up murder," Bishop said.

"It's happened before." He covered the body and stood.

Weber came closer "This guy was a dead man walking. We all know it's a possibility when they play that dreaded game. How sad for his wife and daughter, though. I hope they stay safe."

Bishop moved alongside him. "It's out of their hands now. I know Agent Perez will take diligent care of them. I guess, we should go back to the office and add this on our report."

"Don't remind me. What a harrowing day. With both of them dead, we have a double homicide. And our drug bust case has become colder, unless I find something in Miller's notes to catch the big guy, Santiago." Weber sounded worried.

"His crimes now include a double murder. It'll be hard for us to recruit another C.I. for a while. Our best bet is sending in one of our undercover guys to infiltrate their core as a buyer. That will kick this case back a year or two. FBI has no other choice in this matter unless they catch them on the delivery end." Bishop knew she had to cancel the plan she devised earlier this morning since both Miller and his C.I. had been killed.

TUESDAY MORNING, Weber's fingers pounded the keyboard filling in yesterday's status report with the sensitive details of illegal activities, including the double homicides. FBI's rules required reports filed within twenty-four hours after the initial crime, if possible. He inputted the first half last night and hoped to finish the rest.

Bishop rose and grabbed a sheet of paper from the copier they all shared.

"Did you submit your report?" Weber asked and leaned back in his chair.

She turned and grinned. "I submitted mine hours ago. Last night, I stayed here till eight o'clock and got it done."

"You're really efficient, aren't you?" He focused on her face and noticed her greenish eyes light up from his compliment.

"Nope. It's more like I wouldn't have slept all night if I hadn't. Remember that old saying, never put off until tomorrow what you can do today. I live by that golden rule."

"I'm a slacker. I admit it. So now I'm paying. I think I'll make the deadline, though." He watched her returned to her desk.

She wheeled closer to the computer. "Not to change the subject but check your screen, we have a new message from Director Croft."

"I see it. I'll open it." Weber clicked on the text and read out loud, "*Director Croft has called an emergency meeting in ten minutes.* "Grab your notepad, Bishop. I'm going to the restroom, and I'll meet you there. What do you think it's about?"

"Your guess is as good as mine. It has to be something important."

AGENT BISHOP ENTERED the medium-sized conference room holding her notepad. No one else had arrived. She sat alone facing the wooden podium with its attached microphone bent to one side. No one ever used it. Behind her were five more rows of folding metal chairs. Two black speakers were mounted close to the ceiling in the windowless room's corners along with security cameras.

Weber rushed in. "Where is everyone?" He whispered as he claimed his seat.

"I'm not sure."

The side door jarred opened. Director Croft entered followed by a tall, broad-shouldered, African American man wearing a perfectly tailored gray suit and vest. His expensive black boots spit-shined under the fluorescent lighting. He paused alongside the director and remained quiet. Bishop didn't recognize him but took in his over six foot military stance. Puzzled, she waited for Director Croft to speak.

"Welcome, Agent Miller and Agent Weber." He cleared his throat. "I'm sure you're both curious about my spontaneous meeting request. I'll get right to it." He hesitated and turned toward the man. "First, I want to introduce Special Agent Franklin Knight from FBI headquarters in New York. He's been on standby waiting for a position to open up in our Miami office.

Weber and Bishop both rose.

"Nice to meet you, Agent Bishop." Knight said and slid out his hand.

"It's good to meet you." When he and Agent Bishop shook, she noted his strong grip. His left hand wore a gold band signifying his marital status.

"And you, Agent Weber." Weber nodded and shook Knight's hand.

"All of you can be seated. I have more news." Director Croft spoke in a business-like manner that never sounded too demanding. Bald headed and smart, she never met a more masculine man who radiated such stark power.

"As you all know we lost one of our own, FBI Special Agent Miller, earlier this morning. I've just received confirmation his dental records were a match." He leaned against the podium.

"The coroner has confirmed positive identification now and is issuing a death certificate as we speak. What a terrible loss." He lips pursed as his blue-gray eyes roved over each one of them.

Sorrow filled Bishop. She held her head high.

"Therefore, I'm assigning Agent Knight to fill his position and work alongside you in the Cybercrime, Human Trafficking and Homicide division. The untimely death of Miller has made his joining us possible. He'll be taking over all his files, with your help of course."

"Yes, sir." Weber glanced at Bishop and saw her wipe at a tear.

"Welcome to our unit, Agent Knight. We'll help you all we can." She smiled and meant it, but inside she was shocked at how soon they replaced Miller. The more she thought, it all made sense. She watched Weber remained very professional. He probably found it unusual too, things were happening fast.

"I'm counting on you two agents to help Agent Knight make a smooth transition into your unit and bring him up to speed." He stepped from the podium. "That's it for now. You're all free to go back to work." Director Croft picked up his file and headed through the side door.

"Welcome aboard Agent Knight. Please follow us to your new office or should I say cubical." Bishop smirked.

"Certainly. I'm happy to finally find a position. We moved down here about three months ago. My wife Caroline found a job at a law firm. She's a paralegal. No children yet." He grabbed a briefcase leaning near the doorway and followed them.

"Neither of us are married." Bishop stated. At this rate she'd never be. Her FBI job demanded all her concentration and most of the men she met outside these walls, she ended up arresting. Finding someone she could trust and fall in love with became a chore she rather dreaded. Reliable bachelors weren't knocking at her door. With all the danger of dating websites, she avoided them. Cute rookies still in their twenties flirted with her. But at age thirty-two, she wasn't up to robbing the cradle.

"I guess you and your wife are settling into a new routine." Bishop said and turned into the next hallway.

"Now that I'll be back at work, we will for sure." Knight flashed a wide smile.

"The weather is pretty hot here in July and August, but it cools off with spur of the moment thunder and lightning storm. We're in the middle of crazy hurricane season. After About November the storm threat goes away, and the high humidity really lowers." Weber added.

"I've heard that from our new neighbors." Knight's lips spread into a grin. "Our air conditioner is working full blast these days."

"What's your specialty?" Bishop paused and shoved open the door linking their three offices.

"I'm proficient in computer technology and cybercrime. I'm also a marksman and I'm really missing my practice at the range, since we've moved here. I've worked undercover on several reconnaissance missions. New York has it's steady stream of crime."

"I hear you. Miami does too. With computers and cell phones easily hacked innocent people are losing their life savings, and the thieves on the dark net are the hardest to catch. That, human trafficking, and drug dealers top our crime list." Bishop pointed to the end cubicle. "There's your new office." She stared at him. "If the chair is too low, you can adjust it."

"You guys are so nice. It'll be a pleasure working with you." He headed toward his swivel chair.

"Why don't you familiarize yourself with the desk and computer. There's a supply cabinet if you need any pens or pads. Sign into the usual programs, some may not need a new password since you came from another agency. Don't hesitate to ask if you have any questions. When you're ready, we'll give you some background information on Miller's C.I. They found him dead in a dumpster today. We believe the gang leader named Santiago is responsible for killing him and Agent Miller. Not we have to figure a way to capture him. Most of Miller's other current files are on that desk in the in-basket or the floor next to it. We file the cold cases alphabetically in that file cabinet." She pointed.

"Thanks, I'll check it all out. In a few weeks, I should be up to par on whatever comes our way."

Weber peered at his watch. "Excuse me, I have a report to finish, asap."

Knight nodded and headed to his desk. He sat in the chair with his long legs stretched in front of him. He circled around a couple of times until the seat raised higher.

Bishop had judged right. Knight stood about six foot tall.

She sat at her desk and sighed. Her cell phone pinged twice. A tone she allocated for her brother Jessie's Brain Injury Center. The double ping meant she needed to contact them. She walked into the hallway, listened to their message and then speed-dialed them.

"This is Agent Bishop, nurse Maryann left me a message to call her."

"Hold on." A couple of clicks sounded in her ear.

Apprehension crept up her spine. She took a couple of deep breaths and forced herself to remain calm. His nurse Maryann had been employed there for the last two years and kept her brother towing the line. She also made sure Bishop knew when any problems occurred.

"This is Maryann."

"Agent Bishop. What's my brother up to now?"

"Hey. Thanks for calling back. It all started on Sunday, he kept refusing to take his medicine. I convinced him he needed it, and I watched him swallow the pills down. Today, he woke up all mean and refused to take them again. He shoved me aside and ran from the room. I followed him. He was wearing white socks, and no slippers. When he pushed past an orderly, he skidded across the tiled floor, lost his footing, and fell backward. He hit his head hard. I rushed to his side, but I couldn't wake him. One of the other nurses dialed nine-one-one. I believe he might have a concussion. The paramedics took him by ambulance to Mercy Hospital."

"Oh, no. How long ago?"

"About fifteen minutes. I pinged you when they drove away. I hope he's okay. We can't handle that here. He had to be hospitalized."

"I understand. I'll drive over there now. Thanks, Maryann for contacting me. I'll keep you advised." Bishop hit end call and rushed into the office.

"I have to leave for an emergency." She kneeled under her desk and grabbed her purse.

Agent Knight spun around and stood.

"What's happened?" Weber ran to her side.

"My brother has been taken to the hospital because of a bad fall. He's unconscious. I'm his guardian and all he's got. I will call you when I find out his prognosis and things settle down."

Weber touched her arm. "I understand. Go to him. We'll hold down the fort. If you need anything, please let me know."

She noticed his hazel eyes watched her every move, caressing her with a tenderness she never expected from him. "I'll be in touch." His words soothed her soul. She grabbed her purse, nodded at Agent Knight, and hurried through the door.

WEBER NOTICED the puzzled look on Agent Knight's face.

"Let me explain. Agent Bishop's brother is about eighteen. Three years ago, he was in a bad car crash with his parents. They didn't make it. He did, but the accident left him with a permanent brain injury. One so bad, he lost all his memory and doesn't even remember her."

Knight shook his head. "Oh. I'm really sorry to hear that."

"She doesn't talk about him much. The doctors told her at any time his memory could come back. So far, it hasn't happened."

"Too bad, this job is stressful enough and then to have her homelife complicated, too. What a shame."

"I agree, but Mercy Hospital has good doctors and he's young. Maybe he just passed out from the fall."

"Could be. Let's hope for the best." Knight hesitated before returning to his desk. "Not to change the subject, but can I ask you a few questions?"

"Of course. What subject?"

"The one that got me this job. What happen to Agent Miller?"

Weber took a deep breath. "The biggest case he was handling involved drug runners and human trafficking gangs right here in the state of Florida. After two years of working it, his C.I. provided him with pertinent intel, and we were all preparing for the big bust." He stared off into space for a moment. "Agent Miller went on vacation last week, he had to use it or lose it. You know the FBI drill. He planned on retiring in about eight months after this last case. When he returned home to Miami on Sunday, someone killed him."

"He was set-up?"

"It appears so. The driver he hired at the airport wasn't one of the good guys. The perp drove him to a quiet section of town, locked him inside the car and then poured gasoline over the engine. I figured he threw in a match. The car exploded, and flames burned Miller alive."

"How awful." A look of disgust crossed Knight's face. "Nothing like that ever happened in any of our cases. These guys play rough."

"They sure do. You wouldn't believe what his corpse looked like. I'd never seen a body burned before. These guys need to pay and dearly."

"I'll help you in any way I can. I'll go undercover if you need me too. I know how to deal with those types, remember I worked in New York City with the nastiest gangs in the world."

"I bet. But wait. There's more to the story."

"What's that?"

"They strangled his C.I. a couple of hours later and threw him into a dumpster. One of them set it on fire."

"Damn. That makes two fatalities in this case." He shook his head. "How evil people can be?"

"I hear you. We have a double homicide on our hands. And now, I pity Agent Bishop. We just found out about all this, and a family emergency arises to give her more grief. How much can one person take?"

"I hear you. But as my grandmother use to say, bad things happen in threes."

3

Agent Bishop shoved open the emergency entrance door at Mercy Hospital Medical Center. Multiple eyes gazed upon her. The interior was freezing. She shivered. Maybe the colder air kept the germs down. She scanned the crowded space of sick and injured people waiting their turn for medical treatment; before she hurried across the room to the reception desk.

Her Mom told her long ago that things happen for a reason. Well, if it that were true why did this have to happen after two fatalities at work today? On the drive there, she'd prayed for her brother and hoped he'd be conscious by the time she arrived.

Numb, she approached the check-in area. The forty-something redhead who sat behind the desk wore a name tag that read Brenda. After scribbling a message on her notepad, she finally glanced up, "Can I help you?"

"Yes. My younger brother was brought here by ambulance, less than an hour ago from the Brain Injury Center. His name is Jessie Bishop."

She watched as Brenda keyed his name into her computer. "I found him. Can I see your driver's license?"

Bishop whipped out her FBI ID and gold badge.

The woman looked at it and studied her, before returning it. "Ms. Bishop, your brother is in Intensive Care right now. I'll call someone to take you there. She turned. "Jane, are you close by?"

An elderly lady wearing flip flops walked to the desk. "What do you need, Brenda?"

"Please take Ms. Bishop to the Intensive Care wing. Her brother, Jessie Bishop is in there. Ring the bell and tell them she's arrived." Brenda's eyes flickered back on the screen. "It looks like they are prepping him for surgery, and they'll need some paperwork signed."

Bishop's heart pounded like a fast drum. Chills flowed through her. Was it the freezing air conditioning, or the word surgery? Jessie made it through so many operations in the past, and none of them had brought back his memory. How could he endure another?

"Follow me, sweetie." Jane's flip flops slapped against the tiled floor as they traveled down the hallway. Bishop could have followed her blindfolded. Once they reached the waiting area, Jane hurried over and dialed the phone. "I have Ms. Bishop here for the patient in room three. Brenda said she needs to sign paperwork?" She smiled at Bishop. "Okay, I'll tell her." She hung up. "Have a seat. A surgical nurse will be out shortly to speak with you." She darted away, her shoes smacking the floor with every step.

Bishop grinned, until the sound faded. She chose a chair and ignored the strong scent of alcohol and Lysol. So familiar, it brought back memories of another time and hospital waiting area when her parents totaled their vehicle. Somehow, Jessie had survived in the back seat, but they hadn't. He'd spent several months in a coma in this same hospital. The only difference, she sat in a new wing. Most likely added to fill the growing community needs and handle more patients.

The door swung open. "Ms. Bishop?" asked a tall nurse in a

blue uniform. She held a clipboard and searched the faces of everyone in there.

Bishop rose. "I'm here."

"Please come with me." The nurse ushered her into a small office.

"Have a seat, please. The doctor's on his way."

"Thank you. What's my brother's condition?"

"Right now, he's currently receiving an IV and resting comfortably."

"Is he awake?" Bishops hands trembled. She clutched her purse tighter.

"The doctor will be here any..." The door creaked open.

In walked a short, stout man wearing a dress shirt and tie beneath a white lab coat. He had a minimal ring of dark hair below his bald spot, and very thick eyebrows over deep-set mahogany brown eyes.

"Dr. Stephens, this is Ms. Bishop. She's Jessie Bishop's sister."

"Ms. Bishop, thank you for coming so quickly. Your brother's sedated. We're preparing him for surgery. When they x-rayed his skull, it showed an acute subdural hematoma. Blood's leaking out of a torn vessel into a space below the dura mater, which is a membrane between the brain and the skull. Symptoms can include an ongoing headache, confusion and drowsiness, nausea, slurred speech, and changes in his vision. Subdural hematomas can be quite serious."

"Have you seen his prior records? A bad car accident about three years ago, put him in a coma for months."

"I'll stop you right there. Yes, we have his records here on file and I know he resides at the Brain Injury Center. As far as I can see, he never regained his memory. Is that, correct?"

"Yes, sir. How will you stop the bleeding?" She straightened on the edge of her seat. Nerves tingled inside her. What if he couldn't help Jessie? Would he bleed to death? She really needed her brother, he was the only family member she had left.

"I'll have to do a decompression surgery." He paused. "Let me explain. I'll drill one or more holes into his skull to halt the bleeding. Draining it relieves the pressure from blood building up on the brain. He should be fine after a few days. Then, I'll have another X-ray taken of his skull, and make sure there is no sign of any blood, and his tissues are clear."

"Sounds reasonable. When can it be done?"

"Immediately, but first I'll need your permission to operate. You'll have to sign several surgical documents as his guardian."

"Fine, give me a pen and I'll read them over."

"Grace, my nurse will take care of that. I have to go prep. I'll see you on the other side after the surgery." He flashed a smile and left.

The nurse handed her the clipboard with an attached pen hanging on a short chain. "Please read through these documents carefully and where it's required sign or initial and add the date. I'll be back in ten minutes." She left the room.

Bishop nodded.

Exactly ten minutes later, she returned as Bishop dated the last page.

"Are you finished?"

"Yes. Here it is. Everything looks fine. Now what do I do?"

"Here's paperwork with your brother's surgery code. I'll take you to the waiting room and show you how to use it. Please follow me."

She paced behind the nurse and navigated through several corridors. Her thoughts were preoccupied with Jessie. Grace paused under a sign that read *Surgery B Waiting Room*. They entered. Sectioned into two spaces, it had a small kitchen with a Keurig Coffee maker, and another area with a television set, chairs, and a coffee table.

Hung in the entryway was a flat computer screen with columns listing codes and categories. The nursed pointed at it. "The form I gave you includes a code number identifying your brother's surgery. Use it to check his current status on this board at all times. The patient number list is printed down one side. The other section indicates what stage he's in. Such as the waiting area, in surgery and recovery room. After the operation, Doctor Stephens will call your cell and tell you how the surgery went."

"Thank you, I understand." Last time she was there, they didn't have anything like that. Technology had sure come a long way.

"It makes my life simpler and keeps the patient's loved ones calmer. Please, help yourself to some coffee and if you need to charge your phone there are outlets in the wall. This could take a while."

"I understand. Thanks again." The nurse nodded and left.

Matching his number to the board, she saw her brother waited in the surgery prep room.

Her watch read six o'clock, and she hadn't eaten or drank anything since that chicken sandwich and iced tea earlier with Weber. She dropped a pod into the Keurig and made herself a fresh cup of black coffee. Bottled water sat in a basket, and another one held granola bars. She grabbed a bar and went into the empty TV area. The meteorologist on the television screen predicted a wave off the coast of Africa was now headed toward the east coast of Florida. His map showed the storm would bring heavy showers but wasn't strong enough to turn into a hurricane.

She sipped coffee and ate the bar slowly trying to relax. Then jumped up and checked the board. Jessie's number reported he was in surgery. A chill raced through her. When had it changed? Too bad, now she couldn't determine the length of his operation. But he'd progressed to the next stage. She returned to her chair and dialed Weber. He answered on the third ring.

"Bishop. I'm glad you finally called. How is Jessie?"

"He's in surgery right now with a Subdural Hematoma."

"I've heard of that before. It a type of bleeding that causes pressure on the brain."

"Exactly. Dr. Stephens is operating on him. I just hope Jessie's body can take all this in his current condition. He's suffered so much already."

"I'm sure he'll be fine. The doctor knows what he's doing. Keep the faith, Bishop."

"I'm trying. How are you?"

Actually, I had a quick sandwich and am relaxing with some Tito's Vodka. I toasted Miller with my first shot. It's been one hell of a day."

"You can say that again." She sighed.

"You're still at the hospital, right?"

"Yes. In the waiting room."

"Do you want me to drive over and keep you company?"

"No. I'm okay. I'll head home after he comes out of recovery."

"That may take a while. Call me if you change your mind."

"Thanks. Have a good night. I'll see you in the morning if everything turns out okay."

"If you have any problems call me. Otherwise, get home and sleep."

She hung up and felt more at ease. Why had she chosen to avoid Weber all these years? In the past, Miller would have been her first call. A pang of sadness seized her heart. Tears formed and dripped down her cheeks. She hadn't had time to really grieve for him. Now this. She slipped a tissue from her purse. She had to remain strong for Jessie. She rose and strolled to the window. The sun had begun its decent surrounded in a palette of pink, orange and pale yellow. She stood in the hospital's west wing. Dusk settled in and streetlights glimmered on the busy avenue. Headlights raced by on the Interstate's overpass. Maybe tomorrow will be a better day.

Two hours later, the board's status showed Jessie in recovery. Relief flooded her. She felt like a hundred pound weight had been lifted off her shoulders. Her cell phone rang and played "Hey Jude" by the Beatles. She answered.

"This is Doctor Stephens. I want to inform you that the operation was a success, and your brother's moved to recovery. You may go in there and see him now. I do want you to know that I've kept him quite sedated and will for a couple more days until we can check his skull for any sign of blood. If the brain remains clear, I will bring him around and let him stay here another twenty-four hours for more observation, before I release him. It's in his best interest."

"I understand. Thank you doctor." She stood.

"Do you have any questions?"

"None that I can think of right now."

"The nurse is on her way to guide you to recovery. Take care, Ms. Bishop." He hung up.

Warmth thawed her icy veins. Jessie should be okay. They did all they could. Soon, the door jarred open, and Grace poked in her head. "Did you get the good news?" She flashed a grin.

"Yes. I just spoke to Doctor Stephens."

"Then, follow me to the recovery."

Soon, she sat alone in intensive care aside her sleeping brother. She held his hand and kissed his cool cheek. He looked good for what he'd gone through.

Twenty minutes later, she walked out the Mercy Hospital Emergency door and into the darkened parking lot. Dim lanterns on tall poles surrounded the parking area. It looked so different at night. Exhausted, and ready for a real meal and a warm shower, she headed straight for her SUV. Her purse slung over her shoulder, she carried a manila envelope with copies of the signed surgery documents. Reaching her Suburban, she opened the passenger side and laid her purse and paperwork on the front seat.

She walked around the rear of her van to the driver's door. Was her car leaning? She took a few steps back and scanned the vehicle. Her front and back tires on the driver's side were flat. The rubber edges unevenly cut, draped over the spokes. Some had slashed her tires. She froze and patted her shoulder holster. Empty. She'd left her weapon in the glove compartment. Her eyes skimmed the parking lot. Was someone be watching her?

An owl hooted and she jumped. She hurried inside the car and locked all the doors. Her FBI training and intuition made her take in her surroundings. Nothing moved on the horizon as far as she could see. Should she call her auto club? At this time of night, would they even answer? In her prior experience it took them forever to arrive.

She dialed Weber instead. After losing Miller there was no one else. Tomorrow, the FBI Garage could rescue her car.

SOMETHING RANG AND VIBRATED. Weber opened his eyes. He saw his cellphone wiggling close to the edge of the end table. He snatched it and answered.

"Agent Weber." He rose to a sitting position. His empty shot glass sat alongside the bottle of Tito's Vodka on his coffee table. He'd dozed off after only two shots.

"It's Bishop. Sorry, did I wake you?"

"No. Are you okay?" His lied. His heart pounded in his ears something in her voice sounded off.

"I'm still at Mercy Hospital."

"Is Jessie, okay?" He stood.

"Yes. He's out of surgery. I have a problem though. Someone slashed the tires on my driver's side. I've locked myself inside the Suburban." Her voice quivered. "It's after nine and my auto club takes forever to arrive. Could you give me a lift?"

"Sure. Where are you parked?" He patted his jeans pocket searching for his car keys.

"Near the emergency entrance. Not too many cars are here now."

"Who would slash your tires?"

"That's a good question. One of the reasons I want out of here."

"Okay, I'll be there in about fifteen minutes. Leaving now."

"I'll be waiting."

WEBER GRABBED HIS KEYS, and wallet. He slipped his arm through the leather strap of his shoulder holster with his gun intact, then slipped on his jacket and darted out the door. Bishop's safety on his mind. Had she been followed? Could it be related to Miller's death? If so, it was vital they be extra careful. His informant, Cruz, could have ratted them all out to his superior, Santiago. If there were targets on their back, they needed to know. This may be the first sign.

He pressed the Suburban's start button and took a shortcut leading to the highway. Racing through the green light, he drove into some heavy traffic. He stuck his blue light on the dash, hit the siren and headed into the fast lane. He sped the rest of the way there.

Ten minutes later, he phoned Bishop. "Are you okay."

"Yes." Relief filled him when he heard her voice.

"I'm approaching the rear of the parking lot. I'll stop alongside your driver's door, and you can get right in." He held his breath and raced through the empty lot at fifty miles per hour.

"Sounds good."

When he arrived next to her vehicle, he tossed his blue light into the backseat. She quickly opened her van's door, slipped out and hurried inside. He looked at Bishop. Her face was as white as snow. She was scared, and he knew it. She'd always kept it all business with him. Except when they celebrated with other agents after solving a big case, and they went out to a local bar for a celebratory beer. Today everything had changed.

"Thanks for coming. I'm sorry to call you at such a late hour."

"No problem. It's been a heck of a day for you." He saw the fear in her eyes. "Are you okay?"

"I am now." A brief smile appeared on her lips. She sighed loudly.

"Relax. Your safe. Please give me directions and we'll get out of here." He'd never been to her home.

"Take Highway One for ten miles and turn left on Lincoln Avenue. I live in the Oakland Subdivision."

"I know where that is. By the way, I contacted the FBI Garage and arranged for your Suburban to be towed there tomorrow." He hoped it would remove some of her stress.

"That's great. One less thing to do." She stared out the window for a moment then turned toward him. "I've had time to think while I waited for you. I arrived at the conclusion, Miller's C.I. ratted us both out before he was murdered."

"My thoughts, exactly. This is a sign. If they're coming after you, I'm sure I'll be next."

"I'm glad they only slashed my tires and didn't wait around."

"That's a good point. You may have been followed here." He took a left at the next corner. "Looks like we are approaching your housing area. What now?"

"Go two blocks and make a right on Juniper Court. It's the third house on the left."

"Got it." Soon, he pulled into her driveway. The ranch style home in front of him had a double door entryway, a small porch area and lots of perfectly trimmed green bushes. So did most of the other matching homes. A large Magnolia tree stood in the middle of her neatly manicured lawn. The place suited her perfectly. Warm and inviting. He liked this side of her.

"Would you like to come in?" She slid open her car door.

"It's kind of late. But how about I come over in the morning and pick you up for work? What time do you prefer?"

"Eight a.m. would be fine. Unless you want to come an hour early. Say around seven. I'll make breakfast and coffee to thank you for the ride."

"I can't refuse that offer. It sounds good." He grinned. No one had home cooked breakfast for him in years.

"I'll see you bright and early." She walked up the curved sidewalk leading to her front door.

"Wait," he hollered. Please let me walk with you and make sure everything's fine inside."

"Okay. You're probably right about that."

He climbed out and strode behind her up the walkway. She stuck in her key, pushed the door open wide and snapped on the interior lights. Peering in, they saw nothing disturbed and silence prevailed.

"Looks good. Thank you again. I'll see you in the morning." She smiled sweetly.

"If you need anything, please call me." He studied her face. Color had returned to her cheeks. He stepped back, waved, and headed to his car.

Weber drove home with Bishop on his mind. He'd never had many personal conversations with her at the office. They never really bonded. She'd clung so close to Miller for the last several years and left him out of any small talk. At times, he wondered if she really liked him. He timed his ride on the way home. Exactly eight minutes from her house.

Sirens sounded in the distance. He a right and turned onto his street. A crowd of people had gathered in the middle of the road. Two patrol cars were parked in his neighbor's drive and a fire truck sat out front. What was happening? His heart raced. Red and yellow flames were burning someone's home. The street was so crowded, he parked and walked closer. His heart almost stopped when he approached.

His house was on fire.

Firefighters had blockaded the entrance to keep people back. Two officers wrestled with a huge hose aiming it high at his roof. Clouds of smoke billowed in sky beneath the moon. Ashes floated in the air like snowflakes and drifted down on his shoulders. He elbowed his way through his neighbors standing outside the perimeter.

He neared a police officer. "This is my house. What happened?"

"Good to know. One of your neighbors called it in. They said they saw you drive away. Ten minutes later something exploded inside, and the right side of your house went up in flames. Do you smoke sir?"

"No." His heart sank. All his possessions were burning.

"Could you have left the gas stovetop on?"

"No." Why was this guy questioning him. He needed to go inside and remove his stuff. "Can I go in there before if all burns?" He tried to shove past the officer. The man held him back.

"Maybe tomorrow if they get the fire out. And only when they give the go ahead. The roof could cave in right now. It's a fire hazard. The firefighters needs to determine the origin and cause of the blaze, first."

He stared at his home. Flames crackled and crawled across his rooftop and licked at the sidewalls. Too bad he chose a wooden house over concrete. What started this fire anyway? His mind searched for answers. Until he remembered, the gang member solved their problems with fire. Two people were burned alive today. Could they have attacked his house? Bishop's tires were sliced. They'd planned it that way. They knew he'd be the one to rescue her. They were right. When he left his home earlier, they probably tossed a bomb inside. Was it a warning to back off? Whatever was going on, it put them both in greater danger. He had to do something and warn Bishop.

Weber pried his ID and gold badge from his shirt pocket. "I'm FBI Special Agent Weber and this house is mine. What's your name?" He frowned as he stared into the man's eyes.

"Officer Porter." The policeman cowered at first but looked him in the eye.

"Porter, I demand to speak to the person in charge."

"That's the Fire Chief. He's over there wearing a uniform and white hat." Porter cupped his hand over his mouth and shouted. "Chief London, please come here."

Upon hearing his name, Weber saw the man's head turn sharply in the sparse moonlight. He waved at Porter and strode in their direction. Muscular, he stood six foot four, and had wide shoulders like a football player.

Weber immediately introduced himself, still holding his I.D. and gold badge.

The chief nodded. "What can I do for you, Agent Weber."

"This is my house and it's imperative, I be allowed inside before the whole place is eaten away by flames. I have important documents in there, sir."

"Are they in a safe or lockbox?" He stuck his thumb in his suspenders.

"Yes, and no." Weber pointed toward the front bedroom and stepped forward.

The fire chief's arm clocked him in the chest and blocked his path. "Calm down, agent. I'm in charge here. Your documents will be fine, sound like they're in fire-proof boxes. I'm hoping we stop the flames before they reach that half of the house."

"What if they don't" He glared at the chief. His authority could trump the police, but not this man. If he could only appeal to his senses.

"Are you sure, Sir? Give me one of your men and let him break my front bedroom window. I'll climb inside and get what I need." He pleaded with him. "Please reconsider."

Chief London looked at him and then the section of the home. It stood untouched by the fire that was expanding like an accordion. "I'll give you two men. One to ram open that window and the other to climb in first, and then help you through. You'll have ten minutes to get what you need. Toss everything out the window. Do you understand my rules?"

"Ten minutes from when?"

"As soon as you enter, I'll clock you and so will my firefighters."

"Okay. Thank you." He flashed a brief smile.

"Don't thank me yet. Let's see if you get out of there alive. Try not to be greedy, but I recommend grabbing some clothing and shoes along with the paperwork."

"Good idea. Weber nodded and breathed in the smoky air.

"Horton and Cress, please come over here." Two men sprinted over.

"Yes, Chief." Both men were suited up in bright orange turnout pants and jackets with silver stripes. Helmets encircled their red cheeked faces from the intense heat of the blaze.

"I'll need you to escort Mr. Weber into that bedroom on the far left." His hand rose and pointed. "Cress, he's entering through that double window. So please smash through it and clear an opening. You'll remain guard outside. And Horton, you climb in first and then assist Agent Weber. Once inside, he'll have exactly ten minutes to obtain his property." He turned to Weber. "Pass what you want to Horton, and he'll toss it out to Cress."

"Sounds like a plan," Agent Weber said. "Are you ready? Let's do this."

"Follow Mr. Weber, men." The pair saluted the chief and the trio marched toward the house.

BISHOP SIPPED some hot tea and prepared for a warm shower, her nerves were still on edge. The day had not turned out how she'd planned at all. Home now, she forced herself to relax and would hopefully get some much needed rest. While placing her teacup in the sink, a shadow slinked by her kitchen window. Her pulse raced. She peered into the backyard and skimmed the property. No one. Maybe a loose dog wandered into her yard. She rechecked all her locks. She had a gun for protection and knew how to use it. How much safer could she be?

Time for a shower. Her cell phone played a Beatles tune. Maybe it was the hospital. She rushed into her bedroom and snatched it from her purse.

"Bishop. It's Weber. I hope I didn't wake you?"

"No. I haven't gone to bed yet."

"I have some bad news." His voice sounded so down.

"Go ahead, I'm listening."

"My house is on fire. The neighbors called the fire department while I was gone."

"Oh no. Are you okay? Did they put it out?"

"I'm fine, and they're still trying to save it. I fear it's much too late."

"Where are you?"

"In your driveway. Can I come in and sleep on your couch for tonight."

"Certainly, but I have a guest bedroom." She walked to her front door and peered out. He sat in his Suburban. She hung up and waved. "Come in."

He strode to her entryway with a duffle bag in one hand and car keys in the other.

After he entered, she locked the front door. "Did you walk around my house, a few minutes ago?"

"Guilty. I made certain no one had hidden there in the darkness."

"That makes me feel better. What about your house?"

"The Fire Chief told me the insurance company will probably declare it a total lost."

She stared directly into his hazel eyes. "Are you thinking, what I'm thinking?"

"Yes. It probably was the gang leader, Santiago. We're living on borrowed time."

She tapped her security code into the burglar system. "Tomorrow, we'll schedule a meeting with Director Croft. He'll find us a safe house."

"Good idea. While my house was burning, I worried about you. I feared they head over here next."

His words evoked chills inside her. She thought about Miller and his C.I.'s death. A feeling of impending doom hit her. Were they next?

4

FBI Headquarters throbbed with energy when Agent Bishop and Weber arrived at nine on Wednesday morning. After they cleared the required security protocols, one of the team captains whisked them to the conference room without an explanation. They didn't question the highly respected security operative, he managed the command hub and oversaw criminal activity throughout the state. Agent Bishop figured it couldn't be a debriefing, the Director wouldn't be aware of last night's situation. But she couldn't comprehend their special escort to the conference room.

Once the operative opened the door for them, she noticed Agent Knight seated in the second row. He glanced up from his cell phone.

"How's your brother doing, Bishop?"

She slid next to him. "Okay, but I'll give you the condensed version. The doctor's X-rays diagnosed a subdural hematoma, or in layman's terms, bleeding in the brain. They rushed him into surgery and the operation went as planned. Afterward, they sedated him for twenty-four hours of so for safety sake. They couldn't take the risk of him thrashing around until the inner stitches heal in place."

"I understand." Knight leaned back.

Weber said. "Bishop, tell him about your Suburban's tires." Five minutes later, they'd filled Knight in on Weber's house fire, too.

Knight shrugged. "I have no answers for either of you."

Bishop worried neither would Director Croft.

When the director entered through the side door, she knew he'd taken the shortcut that adjoined his large office. "Good morning, everyone. I'll get right down to why I wanted all of you here." His eyes roved over them. "We have a dire emergency."

She glanced sideways at Weber. Had he already heard about their dangerous situation? With all of his previous experiences and knowledge, he should provide a secure solution to help protect them.

Leaning on the podium, his faced sobered. "There's a crucial threat that has impacted the state of Florida and others along the coastline. Port of Miami's security officers have contacted the Federal Bureau of Investigation regarding a missing seven-year old boy. The child boarded the Imperium Princess of the Seas cruise ship with his family seven days ago for a western Caribbean cruise. When the ship sailed into the Port Miami this morning, he was declared missing by his family before disembarking."

Croft peered down at his notes for a couple of seconds. "The ship's security has done a thorough search, but he's nowhere to be found. There's a good possibility he's fallen overboard. The U.S. Coast Guard and other boaters are searching for him in the surrounding sea. His mother stated she last saw him in the theater around six-thirty this morning when he asked to go to the restroom. He never returned. The family had been waiting there for their final deboarding call." He glanced at his watch.

"Their security staff and other crew members are now searching the entire ship for the second time around. The company has a strict security network installed on all its ships, one that accounts for each and every passenger and crew member. Every person receives a seapass key card and they are scanned into the system when they enter or leave the ship. This provides the cruise line with an accurate photo and identification of who's onboard and who's ashore. The biggest problem for the cruise line is their scheduled to sail again today at four-thirty this afternoon."

"Do they want FBI to search the ship?" Bishop asked.

"Yes and no. Since, the child's missing within the twelve mile U.S.A. limit, that gives the United States the authority to investigate. Here's the shocking news. This particular ship is notorious for losing people. Six in the last couple of years, and not all were ever found." He pressed his lips together in disgust. "The Governor has asked us to investigate this companies cruise business further. He's worried about human trafficking and homicides and how it contributes bad press for the state of Florida. I believe it's a worthy concern."

The door flung open. Croft's secretary rushed in with a thick, sealed manila envelope. "Thanks, Millie." She nodded at him and dashed from the room. "Give me a few minutes guys to digest this information. I knew the courier was on his way, so I started without it." He tore the flap open, stuck his beefy hand inside the envelope and slid out a thick sheath of paperwork fastened with a Bulldog clip. "Whoa. Why don't you agents take a coffee break, and then come back? I'll have to digest all this before I can decide on our plan of action."

They three of them rose and strode toward the breakroom. "I really do need some coffee, but I can't believe this is happening. Do either of you?" Bishop asked.

"I'm not sure that boy can be found in such a brief span of

time. This doesn't make any sense. And I don't think Croft knows anything about the mess we're in. Or your brother's situation." Weber raked his fingers through his hair.

"Apparently not," Agent Knight added.

"How can we broach the subject now?" Weber grabbed a mug.

"After we fill our cups, we'll have a few minutes to figure this out." She poured steamy black coffee into hers and sat.

For fifteen minutes, they all sipped coffee and discussed their best approach. "It all boils down to the fact we're facing eminent danger and our best bet is Agent Perez. She can find us a safe house somewhere out of the area," Bishop said. "We'll tell him about last night, right after he decides how we find that missing child." She checked her watch and stood. "Ready, guys?" They both nodded. "When the time's right, we'll explain everything to him."

"Agreed. We'll follow your lead." Weber winked. They hiked back to the conference room.

Croft greeted them when they returned. "I hope all three of you are ready for this information I'm about to present. These orders are from the governor himself. I'm not sure you'll like them, but I have no choice in this matter." He cleared his throat. "I'm assigning all three of you to a covert mission. How long it takes will be up to you."

Bishop spoke first. "We'll never be able to find that child by 4:30 p.m. How can we figure out a search grid on a large ship and an ocean? There's hardly enough time to get started."

"I agree. Except, there's been a change. I've been informed they located the boy a half hour ago. The Coast Guard found him floating in the Atlantic Ocean. The autopsy will most likely prove drowning. What a shame." He grimaced. "Not to change the subject, but back to the Governor's orders. Although time is of the essence, please hear me out. Agent's Bishop, Weber, and

Knight, you're all assigned for a covert mission on a seven-day cruise leaving out of Port Miami this afternoon." He gazed at them for a few seconds. "And if you're unable to uncover what's causing their problems, you may have to stay on and sail a back-2back cruise for another seven-days."

Their faces blanked.

He continued. "All of you, are assigned to thoroughly investigate and discover what's happening behind the scenes on the Imperium Princess of the Seas cruise ship. My secretary has secured two leftover spacious cabins with an oceanview window. Your new identities and passports are currently being prepared. Agent Knight, I noticed on your resume you speak Spanish. That will be extremely helpful on board. You will be briefed by Captain Mancini and work hand in hand with his security officers. Bishop and Weber, you'll be charading as a married couple taking a honeymoon cruise. Knight, you're a single passenger who wife's recently passed away.

Agent Bishop frowned. She turned toward Weber. "Is he kidding?"

Director Croft smiled widely. "I know this is a very unusual assignment, but no different than when you were sent on other missions like the state of Colorado. We rented an apartment for you two and Miller and your orders were to gather information on a certain CEO suspect and his cohorts."

"Of course, we'd done this many times before in the field, but I've never cruised. How will this work? Besides that, we'll have to pack. I don't own a bathing suit or have to many casual clothes." Bishop frowned.

"Me neither." Weber seconded. "Especially since last night."

"What happened last night, Agent Weber?" Croft stared directly at him.

"I'll tell you after you finish filling us in, sir."

Bishop's thoughts concentrated on her brother. How could

she leave him? She didn't want to share her personal problems till after he finished. If the Governor sent them this mission, they had no choice in the matter. When she originally signed her FBI contract, she promised to go wherever they needed her.

"Okay." Director Croft continued. "There's a healthy credit card waiting for each one of you. The only main problem I see is time. You must board the ship by four o'clock this afternoon. They sail a half hour later." He smirked. "And don't worry. There's Wi-Fi at sea, so we can keep in steady contact."

"Wait, did you say Agent Weber and I are sharing the same cabin?"

"Yes. Isn't that what married people do? We selected twin beds. The mission wouldn't fly if you were in separate rooms. Cruise fares require double occupancy in each cabin. I found out we had to pay extra for Knight to keep this under wraps." He looked at his watch. "It's almost nine o'clock. Go home and fill your suitcases."

"Yes, Director. But first, we need to mention an important matter concerning Agent Miller's death," Bishop said.

"I'm listening." He turned a chair around and sat.

Bishop told him about her brother's accident and the slashed tires. Weber filled him in on his house fire. They indicated their need for personal protection while in the city of Miami. She reiterated that Knight should be safe as the bad guys didn't know about him yet.

Director Croft sat deep in thought for a minute. "It looks like fate has intervened and the cruise ship mission happened at exact right time. This is perfect. You're both getting out of dodge and who knows for how long. And so is Knight." He grinned. "I'll appoint two security officers to keep watch over you two from this moment on. They'll make sure you board that ship. Once you arrive on the Imperium Princess, you should be safe." He rose. "Millie will forward the intel files to each of your laptops with all the pertinent information you'll need." He paused and smirked, "Bon Voyage," before disappearing through his secret passageway.

Bishop rose. "We'll need to leave right now."

"For sure," Knight said. "I'll have to go home and tell my wife. I'll see you two on the cruise ship." He hurried through the door.

"Bishop, I don't own a suitcase and I didn't save much clothing from my closet." Weber's forehead wrinkled.

"I'll lend you one. I've always wanted to go on a cruise." She smiled. "But not like this. I sure hope I don't get seasick."

"There's pills for that." He laughed.

WEBER ESCORTED her back to their cubicles. "Since the only clothing I have is at your place, we'll need to shop together."

"I don't have a vehicle, remember. You're stuck with me. We'll grab the suitcases and pack what clothing and toiletries we have. I'd like to make a stop at the hospital and see my brother before we sail, if at all possible."

"I understand, after we shop at the mall, will stop there on the way to the pier."

"Okay, let's get moving." They hurried toward the exit.

Once, they cleared the FBI protocols, Weber drove through the gate and headed for the town mall. He checked his rearview mirror. They had a tail. One of their own. Extra security would make their life run smoother, but he'd still keep a strict watch.

He listened to Bishop on the phone making plans for her brother in case they released him before they'd returned.

Weber pulled into the mall, and so did the rookies trailing them. They shopped discreetly with the knowledge that those two other men watched their every move. A couple of hours later, their suitcases were filled and packed into the trunk. And as he promised, Weber drove her to the hospital for a quick visit with her brother.

They sat quietly in the Intensive Care Unit, Bishop shed a few tears, but they didn't stay long. He walked her out with his arm around her waist. The port was exactly a half hour away, Weber programed the GPS for the fastest way there. Upon arrival, he followed the signs and got in line to drop off their suitcases. Afterward, they parked in the specified cruise lot.

"We're here. Look at the size of that ship in the harbor. It looks like a beauty." Weber scanned the girth of the large vessel. "Last time I sailed the ocean blue, it was in the Navy on an aircraft carrier."

Bishop studied his face. "I didn't know you served?"

"I don't talk about that period of my life too much." They climbed from the SUV, and he smiled. "Are you ready for an adventure?"

"Do I have a choice?" She frowned.

"No. It won't be that bad, Bishop." He reached inside his jacket for the blue velvet jewelry box the director had provided. "I have something for you." He handed her the box.

Bishop's face wore a puzzled look. She snapped open the lid. Her eyes stared at the engagement and wedding ring for half a minute. Finally, she slid them onto her finger and grinned.

He held out his hand, so she could see his fourth finger wore a matching gold band. She giggled like a schoolgirl. He grabbed the handle on their carryon bags. "Time to board. Let the marriage begin."

She chuckled at his words.

"Follow me, Mrs. Hamilton. Can I call you Liz instead of Elisabeth.?"

"Of course, Mr. Hamilton, if I can call you Russ."

They walked toward the terminal, entered into the single file line, and followed the experienced cruisers up a long platform leading to a large room. His wristwatch read three-thirty and people were still arriving. How many guests did this ship carry? He had a lot of unanswered questions since neither had ever cruised before. It would be a real learning experience and a difficult covert mission at the same time.

Hours ago, they'd surrendered their weapons, and now they followed other passengers through the metal security detectors and bag scanners. Strange as it felt, Bishop entered first, and then Weber. They retrieved their carryons after they cleared the electronic scanners. Next, they entered a room the size of a warehouse with the longest counter he'd ever seen. Fluorescent tubes installed on the high ceiling above projected light on the busy workers. Travel agents checked in ticketed passengers and repeatedly requested passports, birth certificates and other forms of identification, over and over until their turn arrived.

Ten minutes later the clerk said, "Okay, sir. Your wife's paperwork is completed, let's get you registered." Weber smiled at the blond-haired woman behind the desk and wondered how she could remain pleasant after hours of asking those same questions. He glanced at the people lined up behind them, tirelessly waiting. She examined all the paperwork and his check in went smoothly.

"Mr. and Mrs. Hamilton, you're all set. Have a great honeymoon cruise." She directed them to the left side of the room. "See the man standing in front of that doorway over there wearing a blue jacket, white pants and a sailor's cap?"

"Yes." Weber had noticed him earlier.

"Just show him these seapass cards and you'll be able to board. Is this your first cruise?"

"Yes. For us both." He studied her face.

"Here's a lanyard for each of you. Most cruisers wear them around their neck. You insert your card inside the plastic holder.

The seapass has multiple uses. It'll open your cabin door and allow your entry into the main dining room for dinner. Your table number's listed near the bottom. If you order a drink, use this card for payment and also when shopping at the mall stores on Deck Three. Please download the ship's App on each of your phones. There's more info there and read the Daily Compass schedule for reserving shows and other detailed seminars you'd like to attend. For a nominal fee you can chat with each other too."

"Thank you very much for explaining everything." Weber touched Bishop's shoulder and they turned toward the man in the sailor's hat. He guided them into an enclosed walkway where they hiked long steep corridors dragging their small suitcases behind them. The lengthy walk increased in height at each level until they reached the ship's entry deck. Two uniformed men guarding the card reader machines, greeted them. When they presented their seapass card, the device beeped, displayed their photo, and allowed them to board. Weber noted the good security. Their machine's system virtually tracked all passengers arriving and deboarding. When Weber and Bishop finally crossed the ship's threshold, a few other officers officially welcomed them.

"What an ordeal, but we're finally on the ship," he said. "It's really neat. What should we do first?" His eyes roved over the depth of the deck and inhaled the much cooler air.

"Didn't the clerk mention we shouldn't miss the Sail Away Party at 4:30 p.m. I'd like to attend, how about you?"

He grinned. "Yes, and I'm looking forward to seeing our cabin. We'll need to familiarize ourselves with various places on each deck. A big job to take on. It won't be easy to find the bad guys in this crowd."

"Like usual, Weber. Eventually they'll stand out on their own."

"I hope so. The staff are the ones we'll need to focus on. Lucky for us they all wear uniforms."

"Good point, Weber."

They strode along the massive deck amid other cruisers. The ship's center reminded him of a two-way street, similar to Broadway in New York City's Manhattan's Theater District. Their heads turned from side to side, and quite often. They passed assorted restaurants, bars, and fancy mall shops. In the center sat a beautiful apple-red Mustang and Weber pointed. "How'd they get that inside?"

"Not sure. Look at these fresh flower arrangements on white marble plant stands. They're gorgeous." They walked on farther. "Do you smell the pizza?"

"I do, and it smells really good." He grinned.

Above them, electric guitars, drums, and a keyboard started playing a familiar melody. Soon a female singer sang the popular tune, Celebration. People stopped and danced in front of them. "This place is wild." After the brief tour of the ship, she pointed. "I finally see elevators, follow me." They quickened their pace and soon entered a hallway with six busy elevators.

They waited with the crowd of until one arrived and emptied. They squeezed inside with the others. Weber pushed the eight button. The car rose and dinged at their floor. He escorted her off. Crew members delivering luggage strapped on huge-wheeled lifts passed them. They hesitated in the deck's middle. Cabins were on either side.

"Over there is a sign listing cabin numbers. Our cabin is number 8210, it's even, so were on the ship's starboard side. We either go right or left." He studied the arrows. "We go left."

They walked a long winding hallway and watched as the numbers lowered. They had over fifty cabins to go. "We took the wrong elevator. Once we get command of the ship, we'll find an easier route. Didn't she give you a deck plan?" Bishop asked.

"Nope. Everything's on the App. We'll need to download it." They kept up their pace. "This is cabin number 8220, so we're almost there." A few minutes later, they arrived at their stateroom. He inserted the seapass key. Not once, but twice until the green light appeared. "I guess I put it in backwards."

"No problem." She walked inside. "This is so tiny. I thought Croft said it supposed to be a spacious oceanview."

"It's really not that small. My quarters on board that naval ship resembled the size of a closet, and not the walk-in kind. This is just how they are, Bishop."

"I've got a lot to learn." She sat on one of the twin beds. "If it's okay, I'll take this side."

"Fine with me. Our suitcases aren't outside yet. Probably because we just boarded. I wonder if Knight's here. Unless he got stuck in that never ending line."

"The ship sails in twenty minutes, he better be. We'll have enough time to download the App and sign up for their Wi-Fi. I want to attend that Sail Away Party." She opened a few cabinet doors above the vanity. "Here's the safe. I'm sticking my passports and other documents in there. Let's use this code, #1492. Do you want me to leave it open for you?"

"Yes." Weber's cell phone rang. "It's Knight." He answered. "I'm guessing you made it." He listened and then asked, "What's your cabin number? Deck nine, 9243. That's one deck above us. We're on eighth deck in cabin 8210." He paused. "Ours haven't either. Let's meet for a beer at the sail away party. Give us about fifteen minutes and we'll see you there." He hung up.

"I've just downloaded their App and found the ship's deck plan." She rose. "Excuse me, I need to use the bathroom." She entered the small space shutting the door behind her.

Weber located the App and signed up for the ship's Wi-Fi by the time she came out.

"I'm ready for the party if you are." She looked both excited and anxious.

"Me too." He sighed. This cruise would be the best disappearing act they could have ever imagined. Unless his old fears resurfaced. Like back in his Navy days. He hoped for smooth trip, that would keep his claustrophobia at bay. He stared at the tiny room, if only his parents hadn't locked him in a closet as a child. He hated the darkness, and how the walls closed in on him. Their punishment for his bad choices had tortured him for life. Thoughts of his naval service and the three years of sailing brought back bad memories. So, he'd purchased a nightlight on their shopping trip and packed it in his suitcase. What would Bishop think? He'd been afraid this might happen, and they hadn't even left the port of Miami.

WHEN THEY STEPPED off the elevator and onto the open pool deck of the Imperium Princess of the Seas, Bishop's phone pinged. "Wait. I got a text message from the ship."

"*Please note, you must check in at your assigned Assembly Station for the Mandatory Safety Briefing by five o'clock. The muster number is listed on your seapass in the rectangular box stating Assembly Station.*" She pulled her card from the lanyard. "It's D-7. We better do this now. Follow me back inside the elevator."

After completing their checked-in at the Princess Theater, they returned to the pool deck level. Reggae music boomed loudly through well-placed speakers. She scanned the crowded area and saw three tiki hut bars situated in the far corners. From the looks of it, the bartenders served up more cocktails and beer than bottled water. The ship held three thousand passengers, not counting the twelve hundred crew. They're the ones they had to investigate. This assignment might be one of the most difficult undercover missions, ever. She gazed at the throng of cruisers attending the sail away party. Maintaining concentration on her duties in this vacation paradise setting wouldn't be easy.

Several decks below, stewards made the best of what they called turn-around day. So far, not one crew member acted suspicious. An uneasy feeling lurked inside her. Would danger wait until they passed through the U.S.A. ocean water limit before it reared its ugly head in the deeper seas? Most likely.

While the ship still hugged the shore, servers walked in a circular pattern hawking alcoholic drinks prepared by tiki hut bartenders. The waiters attentive eyes traveled over the passengers as they balanced round trays of beers, wine glasses and the day's special, bahama mama. A hand waved frantically at them across the ship. "There's Knight. He's on the other side. Ready?"

Weber nodded.

She weaved in and out, taking in the vacationers. Middle-aged men in swimsuits chugged tall beers on metal-legged barstools. Silver-haired grandmothers hung on their rich husband's arms, while more youthful couples relaxed at pub tables with bottled beer. Single groups of women smiled at what they hoped were the bachelors. Dressed in bikinis and speedos, the tannest sunworshippers rested on loungers alongside the pool. Everyone waited for the first sign of sailing.

They approached Knight. "Good to see you made it. Have you ever cruised before?"

"Yes, my wife and I did a Bahama cruise for our anniversary last year."

"That's good to know. We may need advice on how these ships operate." She smiled.

A server neared Weber offering a tray of beers. "I'll have one, how about you Knight."

"Sure." The young man set two bottles on the table and removed their lids.

"What's the lady drinking?" he asked.

"How about the drink of the day." She grinned as he raced away. "This might be the only time we get to relax and enjoy the ship, right guys." The two partners nodded.

The server returned in thirty seconds. "This is for you, ma'am." He handed her a tall glass with orange and pineapple juice, coconut flavored rum and grenadine. A slice of pineapple adorned the curved edge.

"That was fast, Thank you." She sipped the cocktail and her eyebrows rose. "Wow, this is refreshing."

"Who gets the bill?" The guy waved the receipt.

"I'll take it." Knight pulled out his seapass card and signed the paperwork.

"Thanks, I pay for the next round," Weber said. He gulped his beer. "Life's good so far. Too bad we're here on assignment."

"I'll second that." Knight joked.

The ship's horn gave a long piercing blast, and then three short ones. The warning signal indicated they'd lifted their anchor and also alerted other ships in the harbor. When they initiated the thrusters, the engine vibrated beneath Bishop's feet. The low rumbling below them propelled the ship forward. Passengers stared over the edge at the dark Miami seawater. Music lowered a few octaves. "Bon Voyage" echoed twice through the loudspeaker system. Cruisers, young and old, raised their glasses high and cheered. The vessel pitched sideways and pulled away from the dock. Waves crested with white-foamed froth slapping the hull as it spun a one-eighty degree turn.

Seagulls flapped their wings in the bluest sky overhead and shadowed the ship. Two Coast Guard speedboats equipped with mounted MK-110-57mm turret guns escorted the ship and ensured their safe passage through the long channel of moored vessels. Sailing into deeper waters, the ship increased its traveling speed.

"We're well on our way. So, where we are we headed for the next seven days?" Weber asked.

"That's a good question. We never had time to study the Itinerary. I think it's the Western Caribbean Sea. We'll have to check the app." Bishop inhaled the wonderful breeze.

Knight pulled out his phone and fiddled with the buttons. "Here it is. This map shows each stop for the Cozumel, Roatan, and Costa Maya ports. Since you've never sailed before, this will be your first visit."

"Yes, if we have time to get off," Bishop answered. The ship rocked, dropped, and rolled as it picked up speed. So did her stomach. Her face paled as she watched the ship rise and lower against the horizon, she held onto the table.

"I think, I need some air conditioning."

"Are you nauseous?" Weber asked.

"I believe I am." Her cheeks warmed and her belly knotted.

"Over there is the Wanderer Buffet. They served food and drinks inside."

"It has every type of food you could ever want," Knight added.

"I'm not ready to eat." She rose and walked across the deck as it shifted slightly beneath her. They passed passengers who chain smoked in their designated area. The odor didn't make her feel any better. When they finally reached the enormous glass doors, they automatically glided apart releasing some chilly air.

"Sit here, Bishop. How does hot tea and crackers sound?" Weber asked.

The lingering scent of assorted food inside the horseshoe-shaped room made her stomach queasier. "I'm not sure about the crackers, but hot tea sounds good." He hurried toward the serving counters and returned with a small plate of cheese and crackers. His other hand balanced a teacup filled with hot water, and a teabag.

"I don't know how you take this. So, I brought some milk and sugar."

"Great selection, Weber. I really appreciate it." She inserted the teabag and waited for it to steep.

Knight arrived carrying a heaping plate and his beer. "I'm starving. With our short notice to leave, I haven't eaten a thing."

"Looks like you'll catch up." Weber grinned. He took a tour and returned with a well-filled plate and iced tea. He stared at Bishop. "You're still quite pale. Anything else I can get you?"

She flashed a slight smile. "No, but this tea is really helping."

"I brought along a bottle of seasick pills. If you take two per day, they're good for twenty-four hours. We can share them. Years ago, I had sea sickness in the navy."

"I hope they work for me. I don't want to experience this for seven days straight." She bit into a cracker topped with cheese. "Remember our dinner is at seven tonight and less than a couple of hours away, so save some of your appetite."

Two crew members paused near their table. Their voices rose in an argumentative tone. The taller guy wore a white uniform shirt with two stripes and navy colored pants. He towered over the other man in black pants and uniform shirt. "Samson, you better get that approved by the Captain. He may have other ideas." The shorter man with a thick head of black hair, and darkish skin stood firm and replied, "That's my call. I don't have to ask him." The taller man smirked and quickly left the buffet. Samson strolled off in another direction.

"What was that all about?" Bishop whispered.

"I'm not sure but it shows some ill will between employees. It could be nothing, just one officer pulling rank on the other." Weber shrugged.

"Yeah. Men act like that at times, Bishop." Knight said and shoveled in more potato salad.

She finished her tea and crackers. "I'd like to go back to the room. We should check if our luggage has arrived. Are you ready?"

"I can't eat anything else at the moment." Weber patted his stomach.

"Me neither." Knight stood. "See you both later at dinner. I need to stop at the restroom before I take an elevator." He strode out the door.

By the time they returned to their cabin, two large suitcases flanked either side of the doorway. "Looks like they finally delivered our luggage." Weber checked their tagged numbers, 8210, and pried the door open wide. "You go in first, Bishop." She tugged her suitcase handle and skated the wheels toward her twin bed. Then, she held the door for him.

Bishop examined the closet and drawer availability. "There are two hanging closets and another set with shelves. We should be okay. My clothes are in a garment bag. I can put my shoes on the bottom."

"That vanity has drawers and so do the nightstands. That should suffice for our extra's. I heard they do your laundry." Weber opened his suitcase and set it on the mat provided.

"It's not free, I believe I read they charge to wash your clothes." She unzipped her luggage and tossed aside the flap. As she lifted out the garment bag, Weber said, "Why is there an envelope in my suitcase? They must have opened it." He picked it up. "It's addressed to Russell Hamilton in stateroom 8210."

"That's you. What does it say?"

His fingers tore at the flap and pulled out the contents. "*Mr. Hamilton. Please be advised that we were forced to open your bag and examine it per the ship's passenger's contract. You brought something on board that's forbidden on the ship.*" He stared at her and then back at the letter. "*We have confiscated it. Fire hazard items are not allowed on board.* There's a blank line here and someone printed in blue ink: "Night light. What the heck?"

She couldn't help but laugh. "A night light. If it were a candle and a lighter, that would make more sense. How can a nightlight be forbidden?"

"Beat's me. It says I can claim it upon departure at the end of the cruise." He paused. "They can keep it." He tightened his lips.

"I can't believe it. Oh well. We're learning to be passengers on this cruise ship. But we're supposed to be investigating them." She chuckled at her own statement.

"More like their checking on me. Their turns coming." He threw the letter in the garbage can. "Don't tell Knight about this, okay."

"I won't, if you don't want me too." Why not? Was there a code between men not to belittle themselves. The whole idea was funny on the ship's part. She reached inside her luggage and continued emptying her belongings.

"I see the safe's not locked yet. What's the numbers you want to use?" Weber stood in front of it.

"I told you when we arrived to use the numbers 1492 like Columbus sailed the ocean blue, so we won't forget. I thought you put your stuff in earlier?"

"Actually. I forgot." He stuck his important items on the empty side, pressed in the numbers.

She heard the whirring sound before it closed. "Are you changing for dinner?"

"No. How about you?"

"Me neither. I'm done packing. I'll read the app and familiarize myself with the deck plan."

A knock sounded. They both looked up.

"I'll get it." She peered through the tiny hole. A man wearing a uniform shirt and black pants stood waiting. She opened the door. The name tag on his pocket read Samson, Room Steward.

Weber came closer.

"Hello, Mrs. and Mrs. Hamilton. I'm Samson, your room steward for the next seven days." His wide smile revealed a mouthful of white teeth.

"Nice to meet you, Samson." He shook hands with Weber.

"If there's anything you need, please let me know. I'll be taking care of you during the cruise. By the way, I'm also the floor manager for this section of the ship."

"That must keep you busy. We're fine for now."

"When's your dining time?"

"Seven o'clock, the late seating." Weber chimed in.

"Good. I'll make a note of it. We have turn down service, too. Have a good evening." He backed from the doorframe.

She shut the door. "He seems pleasant enough."

"Agreed. I'll finish unpacking."

"Back to the App for me. After tonight's dinner and show, hopefully, we'll hear something about that security meeting tomorrow."

"Somehow they'll contact us, it's still early."

5

The cabin speaker crackled with static. They both quieted.

"Good evening passengers, this is your Captain, Anthony Mancini speaking." He hesitated. "Welcome aboard. We are currently traveling at a speed of twenty-two knots and will continue tonight and all day tomorrow. We are experiencing calm seas and pleasant weather, and our temperature is twenty-seven degrees Celsius or eighty-one Fahrenheit. Please be advised that our Cruise Director, Mike Ryan, has planned plenty of activities for you for the rest of the evening. There are two shows scheduled in the Princess theater, a comedy act in our Comedy Club and dancing in the many nightclubs aboard ship. I wish you all a great dining experience and hope you enjoy your first evening."

At seven o'clock, Weber and Bishop stood in line at the main dining entrance. Each of them had memorized their history spiel written by the FBI officers who had coordinated their field operation within minutes. This dinner would be their first normal function as a couple enjoying their honeymoon. Tomorrow they'd meet with the Captain and his security officers.

After the people in front of them were escorted to their tables, they neared the Maître D's podium. Weber handed him their key cards.

"Good evening. Mr. and Mrs. Hamilton. How are you enjoying your cruise so far?'

"It's great. Thanks for asking."

He handed Weber back the cards. With a wave of his right hand a worker jogged over as if his life depended on it.

"Thomas will take you to table thirty-three." Weber nodded. They followed the young man to a circular table for eight. Knight was already seated, and he smiled at them. Thomas pulled out a chair for Bishop, right next to Knight. She sat, and the busboy spread a white linen napkin across her lap. Her eyes lit up. Weber took the chair on her left. Five more people arrived, two married couples and one traveling with their mother. They exchanged pleasantries, downloaded the QR menu on their phones, and ordered their meals. Dinner came in four courses. An hour and a half later, Weber led them toward the Princess Theater for the musical performance at nine.

He selected three seats in the center, about twelve rows back. "Follow me." After they were seated, he pointed at the stage. "Look at those extravagant theater drapes. I believe that's a Parisian scene embroidered on lined silk."

"It sure sparkles. Everything here is first class," Bishop added.

The huge curtains parted, and the ship's twelve-piece band opened the show. After a couple of tunes, a voice rang out over a mike and introduced the Cruise Director, Mike Ryan. He came on stage, welcomed everyone, and joked about the twenty-four hours meal service on the ship.

"Tonight's show is Broadway Boogie. The songs are from a couple of different Broadway musicals, I'm sure you'll recognize them." Soon, singers and dancers filled the stage. Their colorful costumes changed often, and their background scenery accented the songs title. The excellent entertainment completed their first day.

They exited the theater and joined other cruisers in an alcove waiting for an empty elevator. After they boarded Weber said, "After only half a day here, we certainly have done a lot of walking."

Bishop smiled. "It should help with the extra calorie intake on our plates."

Weber ignored her remark. Once on their floor, he studied the cabin numbers. When they reached their stateroom, Samson stood in the hallway folding towels.

"Did you enjoy dinner tonight?" His eyes studied them both.

"Very nice, thank you."

"Good to hear. Have a nice evening." He swerved and entered the cabin next to theirs carrying in fresh towels.

Bishop stepped aside so Weber could insert the seapass. It opened the first time.

"Looks like Samson turned down our beds. Hey, there's a chocolate candy on each of our pillows. How neat." She smiled.

"No one has ever turned down my bed before." Weber joked.

"Isn't it funny how all the corridors look similar and use the exact same cabin numbers except for the first digit, which represents the deck you're on. And I've noticed the abundance of doors that state: Crew only or Do Not Enter?" She removed her high heels and took them to the closet.

"Me, too. That couple at dinner told me there is a whole different community below us for the crew employees. They have two bars, three canteens and an exercise room. There's a complete straight passageway that goes from one end of the ship to the other. They're frequent cruisers and said many workers sign on for an eight or nine month stint and hold a couple of job titles." Weber waited until she closed her closet door so he could pass by. "It's tight quarters in here."

"I agree. Here, I'll move out of your way." She slid by him. "Well, I heard the employees have a strict protocol onboard. Excess drinking is frowned upon. The penalties are tough. Many of them need their jobs and send most of their earnings back home to family."

"I'm sure they are tightlipped about the comings and goings on the ship. So don't ask any of them for help. They might report us for being too nosy."

"True." She walked toward the vanity. "We've got more mail. There's an envelope laying here." She swiftly tore it open and read. "It's short and sweet, Weber. We're to meet with the head security officer, his men, and the captain in the bridge at ten o'clock tomorrow morning. It says, take an elevator to Deck four and walk toward the rear of the ship located near the bridge. The security officer will wait for us there."

"Sounds like a plan. My bathing suit is the last thing I have to unpack, and then I'm officially done. Back to FBI work tomorrow, for now I'm ready for some sleep." She used the bathroom, and then slipped into bed. "Good night, Weber."

"Same to you Bishop." He walked toward the closet. "I'll leave the light on in the bathroom after I finish up, if it doesn't bother you. This room get pitch black without any lights, and the bathroom has a step up. Neither of us wants to trip."

"That's fine." She turned toward the wall and pinched herself. I'm sleeping inside a cabin with a man I've worked with for years. While sharing a room together, we'll probably get to know more personal things about each other. Does he snore? What will I discover in seven more days? He's truly kind and considerate at this point. I wonder though, is he afraid of the dark?

THURSDAY MORNING, FBI Special Agent Weber, Bishop, and Knight, professionally dressed in dark pants and white shirts exited the elevator on deck eleven and strode toward the nerve center of the ship called the bridge. Weber's past sea knowledge gave him an edge on information about the pilothouse and chart room. Usually manned by an officer on watch, they were aided by another able seaman, who acted as his lookout and maintained a recorded log of the ship's movement. That's where the Captain engineered and steered his ship's course.

When they rounded the last corner a six foot tall man, who's white uniform displayed his rank, stood against the wall. Weber knew he must be the head security officer.

They approached and the guy said, "I'm Officer Vito Amato, Head of Security." A commanding figure, his deep brown hair had a few silver streaks lining the sides. His name matched the badge pinned to his white uniform shirt. Security patches and two stripes were stitched on his shoulders. "I'm responsible for maintaining safety and passenger control. I also supervise all the security guards who policed points of entry at the gangway gates and tender docking stations. "Glad to have you all onboard and on our side."

His handshake was firm, and his words reassured Weber. High up on the chain, there shouldn't be any reason not to trust him. But Weber knew at times, he could be wrong. It's all about trust. He hoped he found it within this man. "I'm FBI Special Agent Weber and this is Special Agent, Bishop and Knight."

"Nice to meet all of you. Follow me please." He walked them around a curved corridor and then turned left. Halfway down it ended at a flight of stairs that climbed to the bridge door. Passengers were forbidden in this private sector of the ship. Even those on paid tours, it was considered off limits. Officer Amato hurried to the top step, stuck in a key, and then tugged on the doorknob.

They followed him into a room completely surrounded by eight foot high windows. The extended glass framed the panorama view of the rolling Caribbean Sea. "Wow, what a beautiful sight." Weber thought about his sailing on the northern blackish water of the Atlantic Ocean. A depressing scene, not as vibrant or as colorful as this.

"It's lovely." Bishop smiled.

"I'll second that." Knight nodded in her direction.

Weber turned and noted the officer wearing headphones at the helm. He maintained the course as he guided the ship through the active waters. Two other men wearing security uniforms like Amato, leaned against one wall.

"Let me introduce you to my officers." He pointed at man stationed in the corner. "That's Officer Allente over there steering the ship." At the mention of his name, the man turned and waved. "He and a couple other watch officers work the bridge and maintain a steady course along with the captain. Over there is Officer Rossi and Officer Ferrari, they work with me in security."

The two officers walked over to Bishop first. They shook her hand, then Weber's and Knight's. They both stood about the same height, and their name badges were pinned to their top pockets. They wore one stripe on their shoulders along with their security patches. Rossi had a thicker accent and a full head of jet black hair. Ferrari spoke clearer and had shaved what little hair remained on his head. They returned to the side wall and waited.

"Our Captain will arrive shortly," Amato said. "In the meantime, take in this wonderful view."

"It is gorgeous," Weber remarked. He scanned the entire area and compared it with the modest bridge on the naval ship he sailed years ago. Back then, the smaller vessel's bridge had barely any room for two chairs. It's mini compartment used much larger machinery, whereas in today's world this current bridge consisted of streamlined equipment, including a GPS navigational device, and ample radar. Everything had been upgraded in the new technically enhanced world.

The side door jarred open. The captain had arrived. About forty-five, he had wavy black hair, a moustache, and pleasant smile. The only officer on the ship with five stripes, they made up for his short physical stature.

"Good morning, Captain. I'd like to introduce FBI Special Agent Weber, Agent Bishop, and Agent Knight. They are the undercover agents assigned to investigate who's responsible for our past passenger problems."

"I want to thank you agents, for coming. I hope you enjoy your cruise along with the mission." He stepped forward and shook each of their hands. "I'm glad to have you on board. What I'm about to tell you is an extremely sensitive matter. I'll need your reassurance that you will keep this information private."

Weber glanced at the other agents before he spoke. "Captain, you can count on my partners and I to keep this matter under complete secrecy. We are duly sworn in by the FBI, and fully acknowledged confidentiality in all of our investigations."

"I can personally verify that all my security officers have sworn an oath as well. I guarantee they will not reveal your presence." He paused and searched each of their faces. They all stood solemn and sober. "I've suspected for quite a while someone has an ulterior motive to ruin our company's reputation and also mine. They continually sabotage our cruise line." His lips tightened. "Why, I haven't a clue. They may want to damage our higher standard of cruising, or we might be a magnet for crew members in cahoots who use our ship to accomplish their evil goals."

Weber's brow creased as he listened. "I've followed the national news articles in New York, Washington, and even Miami newspapers who've reported what's been happening on your cruise line."

"I have too and I'm not proud of it. They sensationalized the missing girls and awful accidental drownings. I don't believe our ship or crew should be blamed for every one of those incidents. They were out of our control. Unless we have some bad apples on here."

"We're here to help solve these problems. In order for us to begin, we'll need all your files, records, and reports on each of those cases. Once we familiarize ourselves with them, we can search for a repeat pattern. In all honesty, I fear there may be a trafficking ring working undercover. One that has threatened your crew with bodily harm and bribed them not to expose or report them."

"I sure hope not." His entire face paled.

"Do you have a small conference room away from the general public's eye where we can work?"

"Yes, below here in a really private area." He turned. "Security Officer Amato will take you there and then provide you with all the information we have available. There are online records with photos, also files detailed with paperwork and everything our security staff has found thus far. Will you need anything else?"

"Yes. Please prepare a list of all employees who reported or were ever involved in any or all of the incidents. Then, have your Human Resource person check for any discrepancies in the credibility of your employees past history, ones you may not have known about. Like jailtime records, drugs charges or even

DUI's? Mull over those questions, and we will speak later after we acquaint ourselves with the actual files." He paused. "I want to thank you for your complete cooperation, Captain." Weber neared him and shook his hand. "We'll do our best, to solve these cases for you."

"I'm sure you'll do a thorough job. Glad you're here." He paused. "Amato, take them to our conference room B. It's concealed, private and out of the way. It should be big enough for them to work in."

"Yes, Captain." He nodded and saluted.

"You can show these agents the preferred way. Rossi and Ferrari, go back to your normal duties for now."

"Yes, sir." They exited the bridge.

"Follow me, please." The three agents trailed Officer Amato down a couple of levels and walked a long hallway that curved. Soon, he stopped in front of a closed door and inserted his key.

As he entered, Weber's gaze swept the room. A rectangular wooden conference table surrounded by six leather chairs sat in the middle. Plenty of space for his team to spread out their laptops, paperwork, and exchange ideas. A copier, situated on a small shelf sat on the room's left side. An upright bulletin board with several empty tacks pinned on the cork was against the far wall, and alongside it rested a whiteboard with a box of markers. The area certainly suited all their needs. "This space will work out fine. We can start right away. Please gather up those files for us as soon as possible, Officer Amato."

"Yes, sir." He darted through the door.

"I hope the Wi-Fi works better in here than it does in the cabin." Bishop chose a chair and lifted the screen on her laptop. She tapped a few keys and clicked the mouse.

"It should, we're much higher up and not blocked by the many decks." Knight eased into a chair on the other side of the conference table. "I'll find the newspaper's previous articles by Googling this cruise ship. Who knows what will come up."

"Don't bother reading the scandalous newspapers. They'll trump up the matter and write their own opinions comparing the cruise lines. Of course, there's always competition and bad blood between them. Each line has their loyal cruisers that won't be deterred, but people who have never cruised before may think twice about sailing this ship, especially if problems like this keep occurring. Try and find the local Miami newspapers first. I do remember reading headlines about a disappearing girl, recently."

"So far, I'm impressed with the Wi-Fi, it's so much faster. This will be a game changer working here. I noticed there's no elevator for the last few hallways. This office is really out of sight and that's to our benefit," Bishop remarked.

A knock sounded on the door. In walked Officer Amato with a large stack of files. Amato placed them on the table's center, reached in his pants pocket and produced six flash drives. He set them near the pile. "The complete files are saved on those drives. We've had four missing girl cases and two drownings in the last three years. It's averaging one or more per year and we sail constantly, except when we're called to the dry dock. The last time was 2020 right before Covid."

"By the way, my Security Officers, Rossi, and Ferrari will also be helping us out. You can trust them if for any reason you can't reach me. One of them is your next go to. If you know what I mean." He winked. "There's nothing there about the recent child who went missing when we docked in Miami. That's considered an accidental drowning death. We have no witnesses, either. But it's a chance of another forthcoming lawsuit against our company. We were legally docked at five that morning, and by ten o'clock most passengers had already debarked. The parents bear the responsibility of watching their own children, so who's really at fault? It's debatable. There's always a reporter snooping around, and we will probably receive some more bad press. Captain's expecting it."

"I hear you. Thanks for all the information and we'll explore the possibility of each circumstance. It will take us some time to delve into all these files." Weber flashed a brief smile.

"Excellent. Let me mention one more thing. Each week we experience our turnaround day and about one hundred new hires come aboard, and there are several workers who depart the ship for their two month leave or for other personal reasons."

"I hope not the ones who may be guilty of these crimes. Those new workers shouldn't need to be vetted." Knight remarked. "Right Weber?"

"Maybe and maybe not. Time will tell."

"I'll leave you all alone to get started. If you need anything else, let me or the Captain know. I'll check on you around one o'clock for lunch. No one else will be allowed in here. There's a telephone over there, and you can reach me at by dialing #2100. If you need anything before then. Okay?"

"Sound good, Officer Amato. Thank you. We'll get down to work now."

He turned, exited the room, and shut the door.

Still standing, Weber took command. "There's three of us, and six cases. So, let's each grab a flash drive and see what we've got. And then match it to the correct file. Make sure you evaluate everything and create lists about the intelligence offered. We're starting at ground zero right now. I'd like to find some similarities and nail down who's doing this. If possible."

∽

Two hours passed by quickly. Bishop looked up from her laptop. Weber and Knight were busy studying paperwork and jotting notes on their yellow legal pads. She paused for a moment and checked her phone for any texts. None there. Jessie much still be in the hospital. Too soon to worry. His nurse said she'd be sure and contact her when he returned to the facility.

Bishop had four pages of notes jotted on her case file. She craved for fresh outdoor air. She stretched her arms toward the ceiling and yawned. Below her, the ship rocked and rolled, and the engine grinded. She was experiencing slight nausea, even after swallowing two of Weber's seasick pills. How long did they take to kick in? She sighed. The wall clock read five minutes to one and she needed food and a change of scenery.

Someone rapped hard against their door. Knight rose and peeked out. There stood Officer Amato.

"Are you guys ready for a lunch break?"

She rose, "I'm hungry how about you two?"

Weber nodded.

They exited the small work room and Amato secured the door. He handed a spare key to Weber. "This is for future use."

Weber nodded.

"Follow me. I'll take you to the buffet the fastest way," Amato said. He led them in the

other direction and stopped in front of wall that had white painted doors. "This is an elevator, see the call button on the wall besides it?"

They all nodded.

"This is what we call a dummy elevator. It will take you directly up to the Wanderer Buffet entrance on deck eleven. It's sort of hidden because it blends into the wall for us security officers and the Captain. Please take this back and forth at lunchtime. When you arrive, just walk left till you hit the Spa area. This will save you time and get you back down to the deck in one shot. Okay? Please keep it under your hats, so to speak."

"Thanks, Amato. That will make it much easier for us." Bishop smiled at him. She was the first one off the elevator. She noticed the Spa signs advertising their services. They sounded relaxing and wonderful. Alas, she had no time to partake in such luxury. She turned and followed the others to the Wanderer Buffet. The fresh air soothed her stomach, she grabbed a plate and toured the many counters for her first time.

Should she select soup and salad or have some of that delicious roast beef the chef was slicing? She saw gravy and mashed potatoes, but that sounded too much like dinner. Too many choices, but lots of days to sample it all. She grabbed a chicken wrap, some salad greens, and French fries from a different section. Balancing an iced tea, she made her way through the crowd. Most people wore happy faces as they stuffed food into their mouths from their well-filled plates. She searched the large space until she spied Weber in a booth for four near the window. She hiked over.

"Okay if I join you?" She slipped in next to him, leaving the other side for Knight.

"Of course." He lifted his tea and gulped. "This place can be hazardous to your health." His plate held a huge roast beef sandwich with Swiss cheese, loads of fries, and onion rings.

"That's true. I know there's a fitness center down on level five. And I'm sure I saw a walking trail on the app near the top deck. Are we taking an hour for lunch? If so, I'll walk that path when I'm done and skip dessert."

"Yes. Good for you." I'll relax here and check my email."

"I've worn my comfortable flats and I have my sunglasses."

Knight arrived with a plate in each hand. "This food is excellent. You can eat all day on this ship."

"That's the problem. There're too many choices." Twenty

minutes later, she finished. "I'm off for my walk. I'll meet you outside the work room five minutes beforehand."

"See you then." Weber bit into his sandwich, as she departed.

She exited through the automatic doors. Outside on the open deck, a server leaned toward her with a plate of miniature ice cream cones. She grabbed one and proceeded to the other elevator. Entering the car, she pressed number twelve and finished her fast melting cone. When the doors parted, she located the framed ship map, and discovered the path's whereabouts. No time to change, she marched outdoors in her black pants, white blouse and flats and walked briskly in the warm sea air. She stayed inside the guided white lines on the trail hoping to end at the two mile marker.

Most of the path followed the outdoor deck and at times went under an overhead alcove. At this time of day, the strong sun rays made her wish she brought along a hat. Sweat formed on her brow. Not one other cruiser crossed her path. She figured they were all dining or in the pool at this time of day.

Loud music played below her, blending in with children's laughter and splashes in the large pool. She finally heard rubber soled sneakers pounding behind her, someone else was making beneficial use of the path. She swiftly moved aside so the jogger could pass. She only caught a quick glimpse of him in a black hooded sweatshirt and sweatpants. He must have wanted to sweat and knock off some extra pounds. His outfit was much too hot in her estimation. Why was he even wearing it? Running at an even pace, he dashed out of sight. She glanced at her watch and then speed-walked another half a mile. The last alcove ahead would provide some shade. Eager to feel cooler, she upped her pace and reached the outskirts.

As she stepped beneath the archway something tripped her. She pitched forward landing hard and flat against the deck, smacking the right side of her head. Her sunglasses flew off from the force and skidded across the floor toward the inner wall. Waves of pain swept across her skull. Feeling foolish, she attempted to lift herself to a sitting position. Before she could, someone pounced on her back and knocked her back down. Arms covered in a black sweatshirt firmly tightened around her waist and kept her facing the wooden deck. She cringed and flattened.

The strong male pressed her against the wooden deck. Her pulse rose and echoed inside her ears. She choked out her words, "Get off me." Her ingrained training kicked in. She tried bucking him off like a bull to its rider. It wasn't working. Fatigued, she rested and inhaled a few fresh lungsful of air. "Help me, somebody. Please help." He pressed her down harder.

The scent of grilled hot dogs and hamburgers drifted in the light breeze. Chatter and heavy metal music boomed a couple of decks lower and drowned out her cries for help. Cruisers enjoying their vacation were oblivious to her plight. She'd seen no one else on this level. Only the man who had her trapped. Apprehension crawled like a spider up her spine. Her heartbeat increased and drummed against her sore ribs. She wouldn't be another victim on this cruise ship. "What do you want?" It came out in a whisper, as she struggled to breathe.

No response.

Confused, a faint ray of sunlight stabbed at her bare eyes. She inched forward trying to crawl from beneath his weight. Her damp fingers slipped on the deck floor, she desperately tried to escape from her abductor. What did he want from her?

"Don't move," her captor growled. Her frame went rigid and then loosened. One of his hands grabbed a hunk of her long hair and yanked her neck hard. He fumbled with something in his other hand.

She curved up on one side and using all her strength, hoped she'd roll him off.

"Don't fight me, girl."

Much stronger than she, he forced her side down and pinned her body against the deck floor. That voice, where had she heard it? Something pricked in her arm, warm fluid streamed through her veins. What did he inject with? Her eyes closed. Would she die and be tossed overboard? Terror seized her. She wiggled and twisted hoping for a weak moment in his grip. To no avail. Her limbs relaxed. She willed herself to stay awake. Her eyelids became heavy and then heavier. She blinked a couple of times and then they drifted closed.

WEBER GLANCED AT HIS WATCH, an award he'd earned for exemplary FBI service at his last agency. "Knight, where do you think Bishop is? She was supposed to meet us here twenty minutes ago. I'll call her cell." He speed-dialed and listened for ten rings and hung up. "She's not answering." He pressed her number again and stared at Knight across the conference table. This time he waited for the voice mail announcement, and then left a message. "Bishop please call me. We're waiting for you in the conference room." His stomach tightened. "No answer. Maybe she's on her way here."

"Did you call the cabin?" Knight cleared his throat.

"Nope. Clever idea." He reached for the ship phone on the end table. It rang until the answering machine kicked in. He left the same message. "No response there either."

"Go check your cabin, maybe she's ill and laying down or has fallen asleep.

If she isn't there, you had better check the walking path.

Maybe she's lounging up there on a chaise lounge. I know the rocking on the ship's still making her uncomfortable."

"Good idea. I'll be in touch." He left the private work room and finally located an elevator. The walk back to the stateroom seemed longer than he remembered, but their cabin sat completely on the other side of the ship. He passed several stewards servicing cabins and vacuuming carpets. Didn't they ever sleep? He had experienced a similar lifestyle when he served in the navy. Back then, he couldn't wait till they sailed into port, especially if he had leave coming. This trip kept dredging up lots of memories, ones he'd chosen to forget a long time ago.

He arrived at their cabin and slipped the seapass into the slot. The door opened inward. He called out for her in the darkness, "Bishop are you in here?" No answer. His fingers found the light switch and he studied the room for any sign of her. The beds were recently made and there were no indentations like she'd sat on them. A quick peek into the bathroom revealed fresh towels hung neatly. Everything appeared like it did yesterday when they first entered. Worried, he glanced out the oceanview window. Bishop, where are you? The waves crested and fell, but there wasn't any sign of her anywhere.

He exited, letting the door slammed shut behind him. Time to check the walking path, Knight may be right. She certainly had not come to the cabin. While he waited for the elevator, he speed-dialed her phone again. Voicemail answered, like all the other times. He sighed. Should he be worried? Maybe. This ship had a bad reputation for missing people. Cold dread penetrated his bones. He entered the elevator and punched the number eleven. She had to be on that path.

Weber dashed outside through the automatic door dodging two bikini clad women chattering and entering at the same time. The strong power of the Caribbean sun, heat and humidity beat down on him. Squinting, he grabbed his sunglasses, slid them over his nose and blocked out the blinding rays. He'd worn a long sleeve shirt and dress pants for their morning appointment with Captain Mancini. Other cruisers probably wondered why he dressed like that on vacation. Their expressions as he passed, confirmed his assumption.

Signs pointed to stairs for deck twelve and he strode up the steps keeping his eyes focused for any sign of Bishop. Most chaise loungers on the higher deck were empty. The hotter climate had driven the sun worshipers into the pool. He stared over the edge of the deck rail and noticed the large foamy wake left behind the ship as they continued sailing at a fast pace.

He reached the jogging path. Perfect painted lines marked the wooden deck, and he followed them searching for her. He stayed at a steady pace, and never passed another person. Bishop where are you? His head bobbed in different directions. He scanned all the nooks and crannies and marched beneath overhangs and archways. Each step he took, the more his heart constricted inside his chest. His cell phone rang. He dug it from his pocket thinking it was Bishop. Knights name crossed his screen. His smile faded.

"Weber, have you found her?" His voice echoed with concern.

"Not yet. I'm walking the path, but nothing so far." His voice shook as he maintained his fast pace.

"Okay. Maybe we should talk to Amato and tell him what's going on?"

"Give me a more time this path is pretty long. I'll call you back when I complete it. I have to find her. This is ridiculous. We're the FBI."

"I know, but this is a big ship. We may have to ask for their help. I'll await your call, Weber."

The path circled around and two steps later, Weber saw the sun glint off an object near the far wall. He crept over, took out his handkerchief and picked up a pair of sunglasses. He turned them over in his hand. They looked like Bishops. Fear shot through him. He searched the deck floor and found no signs of blood, fabric or ever a struggle. Not a clue anywhere in the eight foot radius below an overhead ceiling that shaded the area. He approached the entrance to the elevator alcove and darted inside, empty. Fear rushed through his body. Where are you, Bishop? Knight was right, they needed Security Officer Amato's help.

6

"These are her sunglasses, I'm sure of it." Weber unwrapped his handkerchief and showed them to Knight.

He gazed at the Ray-Bans. "I've just started, so I never saw her wearing them." His shoulder's slouched as he leaned back against the chair.

"I've checked every place, I can think of. I'm going to contact Officer Amato from here." Weber dialed #2100 on the ship's phone.

"Security, Chief Officer Amato speaking."

"FBI Agent Weber. We have a big problem. Agent Bishop never returned after lunch. I've checked everywhere I can think of. Would you please come to the workroom as soon as possible."

"We'll find her. I'm on my way."

Weber dropped into his chair and pounded the table hard. "I can't believe this is happening."

"Keep the faith, Weber. There must be a reasonable answer on where she is." Knight tossed his pen. "There's only one way off the ship out here in the middle of the ocean."

Weber's eyes widened and he groaned. "Those words don't

make me feel any better, Knight. Someone would have noticed if she were thrown overboard, wouldn't they?"

"I think so. Although the pool music blasts through those speakers. Every chaise lounge is filled with passengers sunning themselves. I heard they claimed them early in the morning. Other passengers are swimming and making lots of noise. And then there's cruisers relaxing on their private balconies. I guarantee, someone would have heard or seen that splash."

A light rap sounded on the door. A key inserted and Officer Amato entered.

"Thank you for coming, Amato. I'm at my wit's end. I've found no sign of Agent Bishop except for her sunglasses. I didn't touch them because they may have a fingerprint other than hers."

"Let me ask you a couple of questions, then I'll know where to start looking. When did you last see her?"

"At lunch, we all dined together. She left a half hour later and headed for the walking path. She's never returned. I first searched our cabin. No sign of her, there. After that, I went to the deck path. I followed along until I saw her sunglasses laying on the floor near that elevator alcove where the jogging trail ends. I hope she didn't fall off the ship?" His pulse thundered in his ears.

"Hold on, I have ways we can locate her. In recent years, the cruise industry received lots of attention regarding serious security issues onboard its vessels. All ships are required to have a surveillance system in place for recording evidence of possible crimes or unsafe behavior. We've installed a fall-overboard image capture and detection system to aid search and rescue personnel and law enforcement. We also have video cameras in places where passengers or crew members have common access. None of them are in the actual staterooms or crew cabins, though. These cameras are focused on the decks where most people gather. They may not always capture everything if they are not pointed in that direction exactly at the precise moment something wrong occurs." He hesitated. "We need to go to the security office and see if our cameras tracked her movements on the path. Follow me." Weber and Knight hiked behind him. He took an elevator to a lower deck and walked toward the cabin marked Security Office. Amato unlocked the door and allowed them to pass. An assigned security guy sat focused on the monitors with several moving views. His head and neck rotating from one camera to another.

"You've met Office Rossi."

Rossi nodded in their direction but kept his gaze on the screens.

He's on duty today. He can help us search the walking path. What time should we start to track her?"

"Maybe around twelve-thirty?" Weber studied the display of cameras as they moved slowly over sections of the ship. Some aimed at the pool deck, others the buffet, casino, and theater area.

"Our panoramic cameras have a 360-degree view, they monitor public areas of the ship and multiple entrances. They're also inside all the elevators, our hallway traffic, and staircases. We've tracked down a lost child or found stolen property this way. Regardless, it hasn't help us with the missing girls or child who fell overboard on the last cruise, or you wouldn't be here." He tightened his lips. "Rossi please bring up the walking tract on deck twelve and rewind it to about noon, so we check for their partner, Agent Bishop. She'd went walking the mile marker path."

His middle camera flipped the images backwards as he reversed the film and the screen showed and the path empty. As the photos moved slowly forward, they circled around the first part of the trail. "What's she wearing, Amato," Rossi asked.

"Same as when you met her this morning, dark pants, and a white blouse. She's thin, has brunette-blondish hair and is about five foot six."

"Great description, Officer Amato. You're very observant." Weber said.

"No, I'm Italian and she's an attractive woman." He reddish cheeks darkened his olive complexion.

"I've got her." Rossi enlarged the view. She seems fine here." A moment later, she disappeared from view beneath an overhang. Pretty soon on the next screen, she emerged on the path and walked at a faster pace. In silence, they followed her for a full five minutes. Until she slid aside and waited as someone in all black jogged quickly past.

"Stop the camera Rossi. Rewind the part where that unknown person runs by her." Amato leaned closer behind his chair.

"Okay, sir." Rossi carefully pressed his finger on the button, moving it snail-like to not miss the black figure. "Here it is. I'll play it frame by frame to see if we can see the face beneath that black hoody.

"Nope. It's still hidden. I don't recognize the guy from his back, I don't believe it's a crew member. Start it again from there." Officer Amato gave the command.

Bishop came on the screen, again. She walked on the trail for at least a full two minutes before she approached a hidden alcove. Once there, it looked like she tripped on something and landed face down on the deck. The cameras caught her sunglasses skating across the wooden floor. At that point, the camera rotated from the scene. They'd lost her.

"Continued on another camera and see if you can find the exact frame that guy ran by and what happened to him."

"Yes, sir." Rossi shifted the screen to another camera and a black shadow hugged the wall. You still couldn't make out the face.

"Okay, here she comes, and slow it down to frame by frame. See that leggy black material lunge out and trip her?

Weber froze. He had no control over what he saw on camera. "We got our man. Now what did he do to her?"

Rossi continued slowing the frames speed. They saw a figure rush from the alcove area, pounce on her back. She struggled beneath him to no avail. Notably stronger, the perp garnered control for a few moments until she passed out. When he stood, he lifted her limp body into his arms and carried her toward the automatic doors. Once they parted, he labored through them and trudged into the women's bathroom.

"That restroom has two entryways. One inside by the bank of elevators and the other door opens to the waiting area for our specialty Sushi restaurant. Their only open at night, he probably exited through the dining area. Let me contact one of our staff." He dialed on the ship's phone system. "Jasmine, this is Officer Amato. Please go into the women's restroom and check all the stalls for a lady with highlighted brunette hair, wearing a white blouse, and black pants. She may be unconscious. I'll hold on."

Weber whispered, "Please find her." Seconds ticked away like minutes, his heart climbed into his throat. Knight patted his shoulder.

"Keep your fingers crossed, guys. I believe we're on the right track."

Five minutes later, Jasmine returned. "Amato, she's in there. Propped sideways and sleeping against the bathroom stall wall. Two crew members are trying to wake her."

"Thanks a million, Jasmine." He turned to Rossi, "Review all those shots again, and see if they captured her abductor. I need a clear picture of his face, one of our cameras must have videotaped him on the jogging trail." Rossi nodded.

"Good work, Officer Amato." Weber shook his hand. "I can't thank you enough."

"You're welcome. Walk with me, guys. I'll call the medical office to send a wheelchair for her immediately."

Weber worried. Had someone tipped off that guy they were FBI? Apprehension swirled in his mind. Fear of what he might learn. Who and why? His brain shifted gears. In such a brief time, he'd developed feelings for her. Their relationship felt different.

Fears of losing her brought back bad memories of his sister, Charity. Only fifteen, the police discovered her drowned body in the lake. At first, they treated it as an accidental death. Until the coroner reported an overdose in her system. Bruises on her neck and thighs helped prove someone sexually assaulted her. Weber parents kept the final results from him because he was only eight. He'd blamed himself for not telling them she'd sneaked out her bedroom window and climbed into a black Mustang.

When he turned sixteen, his parents revealed the real reason for her death. He felt guilty. He could have saved her if he'd been truthful. The jerk kidnapped and drugged his sister for his own pleasure. She never came home again. After years in the navy, he'd joined the Quantico Academy and became an FBI Special Agent. He promised himself to capture predators and their drugs dealers and send them all to jail.

BISHOP'S HEAD throbbed with a terrible migraine. The room spun when she opened her eyes. She fought to clear her vision against the bright lights. She couldn't focus, so she shut them again. Someone's hands held tightly on her shoulders. Was it the man in black? She needed to get away. Her nerves on edge, she lashed out with curled fists and fought the person dragging her upright. Her legs wobbled beneath her, and she braced for a fall. An unknown voice whispered in her ears. She tried prying their fingers from her arms and waist.

"We're here to help, miss. It's all over."

"What?" The voices were foreign and female. "Where am I? Who are you?"

"Please miss, we won't hurt you." A softer voice spoke in a soothing tone.

Her eyes blinked a few more times and she tried to focus. Fear clawed at her inner soul. The walls were so close she could touch them. Was she in a closet? Two women tugged her through a doorway. Water ran. They splashed her face and wiped her cheeks with paper towels. "Where am I?" She studied the mirror and white walls. A toilet flushed and then a door squeaked open. A young girl came to the sink and stared at her.

"Do you remember anything?" One of the ladies who held her upright whispered softly into her ear.

She was in a bathroom, not on the wooden deck floor beneath the alcove. Her gaze searched the small area. No sign of the man in a black hoody. She gasped, her body trembled as she studied the women's faces. "Release me, I think I can stand on my own." They stepped back. She sucked in a deep breath. Numb with disbelief, she shivered.

"You're safe now and your husband's on his way here."

"My husband." She repeated. The ship swayed beneath her feet. She lurched forward and grabbed the sink. Nauseousness hit the pit of her stomach. She remembered. Weber's coming to save her. She'd be safe and in good hands. If only he'd hurry and take her to their cabin. Her head ached deep inside.

The door jerked opened. In walked Weber, Knight, and a security guy. She'd forgotten his name.

Weber rushed toward her. "Liz, are you all, right?" The

women backed away. He hugged her tightly and she slumped into his arms, his warm face pressed next to hers.

"Yes, I need to go to the cabin and lie down."

A paramedic entered through the doorway pushing a wheelchair. "Mrs. Hamilton."

"Yes." She froze and stared at the uniformed man.

"I'm here to take you to the infirmary. The doctor's waiting. He wants to examine you and make sure you're okay."

She stared at Weber, her face drained of color.

"Honey, this is a good thing. It will be fine. I'll go with you." He nodded at the paramedic. "Thanks, I'll see you later Officer Amato." He waved goodbye.

"Now that we found her, I'll go back to the workroom, Weber." Knight left.

The paramedic moved the chair closer, "Please be seated."

She slid from Weber's grip and took a step forward. Still dizzy, she stumbled. Weber caught her arm and guided her in. The medic wheeled her onto an elevator and before she knew it, pushed her through the ship's infirmary door and into a patient room.

Weber waited with her. "I was so worried when you didn't return from lunch. I searched everywhere, until Knight mentioned getting Officer Amato involved. Thank goodness they have camera's all over the ship. It sure helped find you quickly."

He looked so serious, like he still didn't believe they'd found her. A deep trembling started inside her, invading every cell of her body.

"Take a breath. You're shaking. Take another."

Tears formed in her eyes and dripped on her cheeks.

"You're fine now, Bishop. I've got you. He brushed away the tiny drops. She stared at him. "Amato wants to interview you on what exactly happened after you're cleared by their doctor. We can talk about that later." He squeezed her hand. "I won't leave you. You're safe now."

Security officer Amato stepped into the infirmary, a frown on his lips. "How's she doing?" He glanced at her face.

"She's alive. Thank goodness for your help and those cameras." Weber answered.

Bishop saw Weber's hands curled into fists.

She studied Amato's face. He appeared upset as well. "There's not much to go on. The perp disguised himself fully in that black sweatshirt with the hood covering his features, no way I can identify who did this to her."

Weber nodded. "He also injected her with some drug that knocked her out and left her defenseless. How did he get them onboard? Maybe the perp had some kind of medical knowledge. Only your medical team has access to any medication in the infirmary, right?"

"I'll question my medical staff. They all subscribe to the ship's Wi-Fi to stay in touch here and at home. So far not one of them seems suspicious. Although, it could be one of our passengers." He glanced at his watch. "I need to go. We'll talk later." He exited the examining room. Silence prevailed.

"Weber, when can we go to our cabin?" Bishop asked.

"After you see the doctor. He should be here soon."

The door swung open. "Hi, I'm Dr. Cheng and this is my Nurse, Hilda." He wore a white lab coat over black dress pants, and a stethoscope dangled around his neck. "How are you doing Mrs. Hamilton?"

"My head aches." Her fingers brushed against her forehead and touched the dried blood scab close to her hairline.

"First I want to clean that nasty bruise on your forehead." He grabbed some sterile pads from a jar. Already dampened with an antiseptic, he gently dabbed at the laceration. "There's a slight bump and the skin is also broken, I'll close it with adhesive. By tomorrow you might have a black eye on your right side. You took a good fall. I'll give you something for the pain if you like. We'll need to check your vitals, take a blood sample and a few other things before you can return to your cabin." He picked up a chart, slipped on his spectacles and scribbled.

Meanwhile the nurse stuck a thermometer into her mouth and timed it with her watch. Next, she wrapped the blood pressure machine tightly around Bishop's arm. When she finished, she took the chart, filled in her findings, and handed it back to the doctor.

"So far, these numbers are good. I'll take some blood to see what's in your system. You stated you were completely knocked out. Do you remember anything?"

"I tripped on the path and hit my forehead. Someone jumped on my back. I couldn't shake him off. Then, I felt a pin prick in my arm. I know now I passed out." In her past, she'd interviewed women ambushed by predators, but never thought it would happen to her. She was wrong.

"The blood test will reveal what he used. I'm already guessing it's a higher dose of GHB or gamma hydroxybutyric ketamine. It doesn't stay in your system for long." He pressed the stethoscope against her chest and listened to her heartbeat and lungs. She breathed deeply when the doctor requested.

"Everything sounds good. I'll write a prescription for pain medication. The lab will do the test results and Hilda will call you later, You should be fine after the wooziness disappears."

"Thank you, Doctor Cheng. I'm feeling somewhat better."

"If you need anything else, please call. Excuse me for now, I have another patient waiting." He exited the room.

"Do you feel okay, are you able to walk back to your cabin, or should I call someone to wheel you there?" Nurse Hilda asked.

Bishop stood, breathed in deeply and took a few test steps. "I'm good to go. Thanks for everything." She glanced at Weber.

He shoved open the infirmary door and she strode out. As they walked down the hallway, he put his arm around her shoulders. She let it stay. She appreciated his affection in more ways than one. They returned to their cabin, where she rested for an hour.

Officer Amato phoned. He asked them to come meet him in the workroom for Bishop's interview. Once everyone was seated, he stared at Bishop. "Please tell me in your exact words everything that happened, and add in anything personal about your abductor, the timbre of his voice, his scent, or clothing."

"I'll probably give you more details than anyone else you'll ever interview. After all, I'm FBI." She watched him smile. It brightened his dark eyes.

Officer Amato both listened and interrupted often, and then asked motivating questions. Could she see his face? Did he have an accent? What was his approximate age? Quite thorough, he recorded her complete statement.

"Thank you. That was amazing. Now I'll have to find this perp, so I can arrest him, and lock him in our brig."

"I need to mention one more point to your investigation. How did the drug, Ketamine get on board the ship? Were your German Shepherd sniffing dogs off their game on boarding day?"

Amato flinched.

"Don't get me wrong, I'm thankful you found me. But I can't for the life of me think of a reason he attacked me. Unless this guy knows we're FBI, and on the ship investigating."

"I sure hope not." Amato raked his fingers through his dark hair. "Since, it could be a precursor to a bigger crime, I pray you stay together as much as possible so nothing like this happens again."

Bishop gazed at Weber and Knight. She hoped one of them

would be with her at all times. No way, she'd be this jerk's victim, again.

Officer Amato handed her a manila envelope. "These are your sunglasses. We fingerprinted them, but only your prints came back."

"Who found them?"

"I did." Weber answered. "When I searched for you on that walking path, they were up against the wall. I wrapped my handkerchief around them so he could check for fingerprints."

"Thanks. I really need them on this ship. The sun's rays are so strong, they sparkle off the ocean waves, and reflect light back at you. I don't have a spare pair."

"For your information, the ship has a group of mall stores. One is called Port Merchant. They sell any toiletries you may need and sunglasses. There's also jewelry, liquor, and clothing stores. When we land at our first port in Cozumel tomorrow, there's plenty of shops if you need anything else." He grabbed his recorder and stood. "I hope this doesn't hinder the real reason you're here."

Weber said, "Don't worry, it won't."

Officer Amato exited the room.

Bishop's cell phone rang. "This is she." After a slight pause, she said, "Thanks for that information." She hung up. "That was Doctor Cheng. He found GHB in my blood. He encouraged me to drink lots of water."

"I'm so sorry that happened, Bishop."

"Me too, but it could have been worse. Glad you led the search, Weber."

His eyebrows arched. "Anyone finished with their completed file?"

"Nope." Knight and Bishop answered at the same time.

"Dinner's in an hour. Our workday is over. I think we should all go to our cabins." Weber stood.

"I really need to change. The app mentioned the second day of the voyage is elegant night. You'll need to dress your best. Most men wear suits, and ladies dress in formal wear. They'll be taking pictures at dinner and on the main deck."

"I brought along a sports coat and tie."

"That should work," Knight said.

"One more thing team, avoid the cameras. Photos are the last thing we need for obvious reasons. As usual, maintain a low profile. Of course, this is a perfect time to check out the staff as the photographers come out like vultures wanting to snap your picture." Weber pulled open the door.

"Waiters will be serving champagne after dinner on the main deck, and usually everyone shows up there for the dancing music. Time to go." Bishop walked out first.

Weber exited last and locked the door behind him.

They strolled the long hallway to the other set of elevators. "Our cruise director, Mike Ryan is supposed to be one of the best on all the ships, I overheard two women in the bathroom talking."

Two hours later, Weber led Bishop to the dining room, and they waited behind a few others. Playing a married couple had its ups and downs, keeping their names straight was an ordeal.

"Welcome, Mr. and Mrs. Hamilton. You both look wonderful tonight. I hope you enjoy the fine meal our chef has prepared for elegant night." He turned and gestured at a waiter to escort them to their table.

As they approached, Weber noticed Knight was already seated with the other two couples and their mother. They were chattering about their first full sea day. They were the last to arrive because Bishop had a problem strapping her dress shoes.

The waiter pulled out Bishop's chair and she sat. He spread a white linen napkin across her lap, as usual. She flashed a quick smile and Weber couldn't help but notice how great she looked in the black form fitting dress. Sequins stitched around her neckline and sleeves glimmered beneath the dining room lighting. Soft piano music played in the background.

He'd wore his new dark gray suit and matching silk tie. Too bad this was play-acting for them both. He'd love to compliment her for real. His attraction for her had grown in the last twenty-four hours. When they were out of their workroom, they behaved naturally. The cruise life had a way of relaxing him. He opened the QR menu on his phone app. It offered great choices for the second night in a row. What's not to like? Deep down inside, he found it hard to concentrate on their covert mission, as he dined with her at this fancy table adorned with gold trimmed plates, and a pink and white carnation centerpiece.

The server circled the table taking their meal selection, while his helper filled their water glasses. Weber ordered lobster, salad, and French onion soup. Bishop didn't care for fish and asked for the prime rib, baked potato, and salad. He'd learned more about her in these last two days than the whole three years they'd worked together. He gazed away and wondered why this woman was getting under his skin.

"What did you two do today?" A male voice across from him asked. He caught Weber off guard. "I'll let my wife answer that." He glanced over at Bishop. She had applied extra makeup on her forehead and combed her bangs over the injured area and black eye. Nicely concealed. No one would notice anything.

"We went to the Solarium and into the hot tubs and relaxed. We both brought our iPads loaded with books to read. So, we sat by the pool and dined at their bistro for lunch. How about you?" She stared back at him, a particularly good liar for sure. She really paid attention at the great training sessions offered by Quantico's Academy.

Bishop had given a genuine spiel and saved him from fumbling with his words. An excellent job. She certainly knew the ins and outs of the ship. He had no idea what the Solarium was or the food place either. The hot tubs and pool sounded like a good place to unwind. He hoped they'd get a chance to relax in them for real.

Flashes of light, laughter and conversation filled the dining room as photographers went table to table taking photos of couples and friends who sailed together. Right before they approached their table, Bishop jumped up and excused herself for a fast bathroom break. Another good move on her part. Her photograph was avoided. Quick thinking, she kept impressing him daily. Knight simply held up his hand in front of his face and refused, said he was traveling alone, and photos weren't necessary.

Waiting for Bishop's return, Weber noticed the sun was lowering into the bluest ocean. When she sat, he pointed it out. "There's an amazing sunset on the west side of the ship." Conversation ceased as everyone at their table twisted in that direction.

"It's quite beautiful, Web...Russ." It sounded as though she'd almost slipped but ended covering it up well.

"I've heard the best sunsets are the ones that melt into the sea's waves. Now we've experienced it on our first cruise." He stared at her.

Her eyes met his and he sunk into them.

He'd hoped they solved the Imperium Princess crimes before the final night aboard, so he could walk off the ship and continue their budding relationship on dry land.

7

On Friday morning, the ship sailed in and docked at its first port, Cozumel, Mexico. Bishop, Weber, and Knight were reading and sorting through documents in the work room, while other vacationing passengers disembarked the ship for daily tours, beaches, or island shopping.

"Is anyone ready to discuss their case findings?" Bishop had sorted her information into two piles. She studied her partners waiting for an answer. Absorbed in their files, Agent Weber and Knight sat silent in the small quarters loaned to them by the captain. They both glanced up at the same time.

"I'll take that as a no. I'm ready. I chose a flash drive with their first case. If you're willing to listen, I'll start."

"Go ahead, Bishop." Weber set his pen on the table and crossed his arms.

Knight yawned and leaned back into his chair. "I'm all ears."

"In September 2019 on one of their seven-day cruises, a fifteen-year-old girl named Sarah Anderson went missing at the San Juan, Puerto Rico port stop. The mother alerted security after frantically searching the buffet and teen center about five hours later. She told the authorities Sarah went to the Wanderer

Buffet for breakfast around eight a.m. and then signed in at the teen center at nine. When she went to check on her for lunch she wasn't there. Records confirmed she never use her seapass to exit or board back on the ship.

The ship's terminal building had 360 cameras installed that captured their family signing in at the check-in counter on boarding day. Their internal computer stored copies of their travel documents presented at boarding. The mother kept their original passports in the cabin's safe and produced her daughters when security requested it. They interviewed her thoroughly with questions like who her daughter had associated with on the ship? If she ever ran away from home? Did they have a disagreement that morning?" Bishop folded back a page on her pad and then went on. "I've discovered security has a special protocol system set up for any missing or lost cruisers. Once reported, they examined the entire cruise ship and check all their film. No one is allowed off or on. Stewards are required to enter every cabin and then all the entertainment venues. They found no sign of the girl. In the end, they reported her missing to the San Juan Police Department and the ship sailed on."

"What else could they do? They're in charge in the territorial waters under Maritime Law, until they reach the United States port." Weber added. "Have you made a list of all the crew and people involved in that search?"

"Of course. She's the first girl missing from this cruise line. Sarah's photo shows an extremely attractive, Caucasian girl, slim with long black curls." She held it up for them to view before continuing. "She spent her free time with other teens in the designated youth area. Every one of those teens were eventually interviewed. They confirmed she'd played video games in the supervised Junior Cruiser section of the ship. No one described her as a loner, but she stayed with the crowd in the center and made several friends. They have photos of her with the others on sea days when the camera randomly recorded them during sailing. But not one crew member working at that morning's breakfast could verify they saw her in the Wanderer Buffet, nor could the teens in the center. Maybe she didn't really go to either place or lied to her Mother. That age group is hard to gauge. A savvy, twenty something guy could have easily taken advantage of her."

"That's so true." Knight added.

"She probably met the wrong person on the ship. Someone who flattered her, gained her confidence, and asked her to meet him the morning they landed in port. He and an accomplice somehow managed to whisk her off the ship and into a ring of human traffickers. She was a perfect candidate for the cartel." Bishop slipped her paperwork into the manila file. "My theory is they used her seapass and took her legally off the ship. She never returned, because someone must have been in cahoots with another person in the computer room, who was paid well to immediately delete her exit from the system and also their backup cameras. No one would know differently."

"There's no telling where she could be currently. That was four years ago. She'd be nineteen by now if she's still alive. We probably won't find her and unless we discover the predators and get lucky." Weber scratched his forehead. "Go on to the next file. I'm almost done with this one."

"Do you think there are stalkers on this ship?" Knight asked.

"Certainly. Remember the five "P's" rule in human trafficking. Let me remind you. The Pretender makes their victims believe they are so worthy, the Provider takes care of them, the Promiser provides cash and presents, the Protector shows them their physical powers to safekeep them and that's how they influence them. If none of those traits work, then the Punisher-inflicts violence and threats to control them."

"Bishop, you are one smart cookie." Knight complemented her.

She continued. "Let's keep our eyes peeled at all times for young teenage girls and boys who appear with the same crew workers who may have befriended them. It's farfetched, but there are not as many teens onboard as there are older folk. Next time we're in the theater, I want you to take a good look around at all the silver, gray and white haired people. These travelers are the ones who keep these ships sailing with their healthy 401k's and retirement packages. They are repeat cruisers with an established rank, and most ship lines cater to them. They achieve status the more days they travel, and are rewarded with free drinks coupons, gifts, and other benefits of special treatment."

"That's good preliminary information, Bishop. I hope when we all compare the dates, time, and names listed in each one of these files of who notified or worked with security, we'll recognize someone that could be an informant working both sides." Weber closed his file. "It has to be lunchtime, my stomach is growling."

Knight yawned and stared at his wrist. "My watch says ten minutes to noon. We might as well, lock up and head to the Wanderer Buffet on our private express elevator." He stood. "And Bishop, please stay with us this time. Someone out there may still be watching you."

She shivered. His remark sent adrenalin racing through her veins. "I've never had anything like that happen to me and I don't ever want to go through it again." Her eyes focused on Weber. If he hadn't searched for her yesterday, she might have been thrown overboard, eaten by sharks, or drowned by now. He was her knight in shining armor. The thought shot warmth flowing through her. Something tingled in the pit of her stomach, as if there was some sort of invisible bond forming between them. She was falling for him. A rush of pink stained her cheeks just thinking about it. They were getting closer.

They waited for the crew elevator's arrival and entered when the door's slid open. The car whisked them to the buffet level where they blended into the hide of activity near the entrance. Ahead of them, a man wearing a uniform polo and white shorts yanked on the wrist of a younger woman. Dressed in a skimpy turquoise sundress, her lengthy black curls danced atop her bare sunburned shoulders. He held onto her tightly.

Bishop glanced sideways at the girl who was probably about fourteen. Her pretty tanned face wore a look of despair. The guy must have noticed. She heard him say, "If you really want to go back to the room to rest, I guess we can skip lunch today." He turned and faced the alcove of elevators. When one of their doors slid apart, he hustled the girl inside, and they disappeared. Bishop frowned. What was that all about?

The three of them blended into the crowd until they reached the attendant on duty.

A very handsome young man with a great tan, stood in the doorway and greeted them with his accented singsong statement. "Washy, washy." His keen eyes guarded the buffet entryway, and he controlled all the diners. He made everyone washed their hands before they came in and touched the food serving utensils. Hand sanitizer machines had been installed at various places on the ship. Bishop knew all cruise ships feared a Norovirus outbreak. Very contagious, this crucial hand washing method helped the ship protect themselves and their passengers. Automatic soap dispensers hung over the faucets and paper towels slid out conveniently from metal boxes attached to the wall.

"I'm making note of that last guy we saw with that younger girl, he seemed awful hotheaded and much older." Bishop washed her hands. "Plus, he wore a shirt with the ship's logo. I couldn't quite see his name on the pocket."

"We have to be incredibly careful Bishop, not to reveal the reason we're here. If we challenge someone, it might blow our cover. She could be his teenage daughter or his sister. That's a difficult age." Weber dried his hands and tossed the damp paper towel into a waste can. "You know what they say, don't assume anything. Sometimes things aren't what they appear." He stared into her eyes and grinned.

"I got you, Weber. But most times my intuition is correct."

"You'll win this fight, Bishop." Knight smirked. "I'm a married man and I know that better than either of you. You learn not to doubt your wife. Women are usually right." He winked at Weber.

Bishop claimed a table for four on the buffet's portside. At this time of day everyone showed up hungry and seats were far and few. Especially the tables with the best scenic views hugging the huge windows while they were docked. Bishop sat and waited while Weber and Knight hurried to the counters. She stared at the choppy turquoise ocean waves sending their white foamy tips upward toward the sky. The few clouds in the distance looked like whipped meringue toppings as they slowly floated by. Blackish remnants of smoke drifted behind from another parked ship's smokestack. They signaled and navigated into the deeper water. Bishop's gaze returned to the buffet area. Passengers walking by with two heaping plates. How could they eat all that?

All of a sudden, a screeching alarm blared over, and over!

Fear settled in her chest. Chills traveled through her. The loudspeakers boomed with static. An urgent announcement echoed in the entire buffet. "Bravo, Bravo, Bravo, Deck Five, Aft." It repeated, "Bravo, Bravo, Bravo, Deck Five, Aft." Some of the cruisers passengers paused and stood still like statues. Silence reigned for half a minute. Soon voices whispered and the Wanderer Buffet changed into a high octave buzz.

"What's happening." Knight shouted as he returned with an empty plate. His eyes focused on people fleeing in different directions. A constant onslaught of intermittent warnings blasted through the intercom.

Weber returned to the table. "That's the fire alarm code. I've heard that same phrase announced many a time in the navy. It could be genuine unless someone triggered the switch by accident. We'll need to treat it as real. Since we're on deck nine, let's wait it out. The Captain will take over and inform us if there's any need to panic and if so send us to our muster stations. It's not a suitable time to get inside an elevator or take a stairwell.

His nearness calmed Bishop and made her feel safer. "I'm worried about the files and our computers." That's the last thing we need is to lose important internal information and the challenging work we've completed so far.

Weber faced her. "I think they'll be safer there below the bridge."

"What if they're the reason there's a fire. Do you think someone knows why we're on the ship and is trying to stop us? Could there be a leak?"

Weber shrugged. He set down his plate and wiped sweat off his brow. "I don't know, but I'm sure we'll find out. Nothing we can do about it."

She scanned the crowd, searching for a sign of anyone watching or waiting for them to make a move. Thoughts of her brother, Jessie, filler her mind. She needed to stay alive for his sake. Who could look after him if something happened to her? The state? If only she could hear his voice and be reassured, he was well. When they resolved this situation, she'd call the nurse and get an update.

She noticed Knight kept watch on the buffet area with an

avid interest. He and Weber leaned back against the windows. All unarmed FBI agents, how could they ever protect themselves in the middle of the sea? She hadn't thought of that when they locked their weapons in the FBI range safe.

"I don't smell smoke or see any flames do either of you?"

"Nope." Weber answered. Two security men in uniforms, followed by Samson sprinted

past. "There goes our room steward, he must be certified to help out with emergencies."

Bishop turned and saw Office Amato in a heated conversation with another officer. Then he headed their way.

"Are you all okay?" His dark eyes darted over them.

"So far," Bishop answered and noted the genuine concern in eyes.

"My men are continuing the search, so far, we haven't found any fire. Please remain here and as soon as they're finished an all clear will sound. You are not in danger at this level. We haven't found a spark." He hesitated, "I have to go. We'll speak later."

"Lets us know what you find out," Weber said and tightened his jaw.

Amato saluted them and hurried toward the outdoor pool area.

She shivered. Since someone tried to kidnap her yesterday, could this fire alarm just be a coincidence. A sea of faces swam by. Other people's lives were in danger, too. The constant ringing echoed in her ears. She covered them. When the noise finally ceased, she gazed at Weber and Knight. They slouched in their chairs and wore neutral expressions.

After a taunt silence, a bass-toned voice boomed through the speaker system. Everyone in the buffet simmered down. "This is your Captain speaking. My security officers have determined there's no fire on board the Imperium of the Seas. We've experienced a false alarm. In the meantime, I'm requesting all passengers to remain in their current location for the next ten minutes, so not to clog the stairwells or elevators." He paused. "I repeat there's no fire on Deck Five or anywhere else on the ship. My staff will need time to return to their positions and then all onboard activities scheduled will continue as normal. I apologize for the delay and wish you all a pleasant afternoon."

"Do you think this was a prank or someone needed a diversion?" Bishop asked.

Weber squinted at her as if making mental calculations.

"I'll vote for a prank," Knight answered.

"Maybe a sinister act for an unknown reason." Weber's cool undertones confirmed he thought something was up.

They sipped their iced tea until Weber pointed at passengers making food choices at the counters. "Time to fill our plates, before something else happens."

THAT EVENING, after dinner and a comedy show, Weber escorted Bishop to their room. They discussed the comedian. "He had the best jokes, ones I've never heard before. I haven't laughed that much in a long time. I like the clever way, he made fun of cruising."

"I can't remember attending a show like that on land in years. His impersonations of famous people were impressive." Bishop smiled.

He sighed and dropped on the edge of his twin bed. A whoosh of air sounded. "I guess I ate too much already and gained weight." He laughed it off.

"It's probably an old mattress that needs updating. These cabins are constantly filled weekly." She sat and kicked off her heels.

"Thanks for the confidence builder statement. I'm glad to see you're back to normal."

Knuckles thudded against their door.

"Who can that be?" Weber rose and peered out. "It's Amato." He twisted the lock and opened it.

"May I come in? I need to discuss something with you both."

"Sure." Weber shut the door behind him.

"I want to pick your brain. We have a problem. A female about fourteen is missing. Her mother can't find her anywhere and the girl hasn't returned to their room. She's frantic."

"Oh, no. When did she last see her?"

"When she took her daughter to the teen center around 7:00 p.m. She signed her in and planned on picking her up right after the comedy show."

"Where's the teen center?" Bishop asked.

"On deck eleven near the arcade and ice cream place. When she first arrived, there were thirty or so kids already there and four crew members supervising. She learned teens had to be signed in by an adult, and none of them could leave without being signed out. The mom agreed and told them she'd be back around 9:00 p.m." He leaned against the wall. "When she returned only ten kids were left, but her daughter wasn't one of them. She asked a crew member where she could be. They said a few kids walked over to the ice cream shop around the bend for a soft drink, and thought she went with them. The mother dashed to the shop. Her daughter wasn't there. None of the other kids knew her whereabouts." He sighed. "Some of the crew members she spoke with told her not to worry, that she'd probably show up later. Worried, the mother felt they weren't taking her seriously. This happens a lot, the older kids just run off to play games in the arcade or go out on deck and take a walk. She's probably doing just that. But when this woman started disturbing our other passengers asking for their help.

Someone complained. A crew member asked her to return to her cabin and wait. She didn't much care for that remark. That's when security got involved. Now it's up to me to find her. I'm hoping for your help."

Weber looked at Bishop and answered, "Certainly. But you already know, we have to remain anonymous, or our cover will be completely blown."

"Yes, sir." Amato nodded.

"Can the mother identify any of the teens she saw her with earlier?" Weber slid on his shoes and Bishop, her flats.

"She noticed a few boys staring at her daughter on the deck during the sail away party, and then again tonight in the main dining room. She's in my office notifying her husband and the other couple their cruising with."

"We can help, discreetly. Provide me with a photo of the girl and her description. We'll go wander around that deck and no one will be the wiser. Check with your staff at the teen center and ask for the boy names signed-in on tonight's list. Match them to their cruise seapass cards and bring up their photos. Maybe the mother will recognize those guys. If so, see if you can locate them.

"Thanks for the useful information. I'll send what you need, shortly. "

"We'll wait for your text message. I also suggest asking the mom if her daughter made close friends with any of the girls. Then interview them. We'll visit the video arcade area, teen center and ice cream place and keep our eyes and ears open."

"Sounds good. Those kids won't worry about you, but if they see my uniform security guys come out in full force, we'll never find her."

"I understand."

Amato exited their cabin.

"Should we bother, Knight?" Bishop gazed at Weber.

"Nope. They say three's a crowd. We'll stand out enough on that floor. Let's hit that bar on the main deck first, get some champagne and hang out on the teens deck like we're lost. You'll need to giggle a lot as if you're tipsy."

"Good idea, Weber." She grinned.

Weber locked the cabin, and they took the closest elevator. Once on deck three, they heard a male singer accompanied by a rock band, belt out the Rolling Stones song, Satisfaction. Several cruisers in the audience sang along. They approached the busy bar, and he shouted out his order.

The ship scheduled its dance parties around nine-thirty or later. Tonight, the party patrons dressed in assorted white outfits and danced on the raised acoustical absorbing floor. Weber knew from his tour of duty, ships at sea vibrated as much as buildings during an earthquake. The constant motion sent vibrations throughout the structure of the ship and to keep everything intact, stabilizers were installed.

He handed Bishop a champagne flute filled with a light-golden liquid. "Cheers," he said. They clinked glasses. He stared into her emerald eyes, wishing this weren't a fake honeymoon. He sighed. "Let's return to the elevator."

At the eleventh floor, they walked out hand in hand and paused outside the noisy game room. They took in the teenagers at different video game machines enticed by the synthesized musical soundtracks and strobing lights. Seapass cards swiped rapidly as the arcade machine chiptunes teased them to play more.

They strolled on and visited the ice cream shop. Two teen girls stood in line at the counter.

"If I didn't have this crystal glass of champagne in my hand, I'd be picking out my favorite ice cream, mint chocolate chip."

"Maybe the next time we're up here," Weber answered. It was his first choice too.

Bishop laughed and sipped from her flute. "Want to go outside on the deck?"

They moved closer causing the automatic doors to part. A slight breeze sent a burst of cool salty air their way. Weber walked onto the deck and halted at the white rail. Bishop followed. Lighting hanging from the ship's rafters illuminated the wooden deck like a candelabra.

"What a magnificent view." He admired the sparkling stars and new moon high above in the night sky, and then he stared at the rolling night version of the black Caribbean sea. Water churned and small wave caps slapped the portside in an uneven rhythm.

His phone pinged once. A text had arrived from Officer Amato. "He's sent a description and a photo of the missing girl, Bishop. She's blonde, about five foot two, blue eyes and wearing white denim jeans and a silky white blouse."

"Good to know." Should we go back to the arcade and check again?"

Footsteps sounded around the bend where the ship widened.

"Hold on," he whispered.

They waited and heard them halt. Soon, male voices conversed. He stared into Bishop's green eyes and put his finger to his lips.

She acknowledged his signal.

"What a night. Did you have a fun time?" A young male voice joked.

" Yeah. Except, I'm worried about the girl. I can't wake her up. I may have put too many sleeping pills in her drink."

"We'll have to get her out of my cabin, before my parents come back from that white party. Where can we hide her?"

"I'm not sure, yet. Do you think she can walk?"

"Maybe. Or we'll prop her up on. If we meet anyone in the

hallway, you can push her against the wall and kiss her. I'll pretend I'm digging for my seapass."

"I hope it doesn't come to that. Where should we take her?"

"Do you remember that Crew Only door on deck one? It's sort of hidden right near the elevators we took before getting off in port today."

"Yeah, I know where you're talking about."

"When we reboarded, a guy went through it, and I caught a glimpse of a long hallway. Let's put her there. Then, jump right back on an elevator."

"Should we go now?"

"We better. Her mom mentioned picking her up at nine. Its later, then that. She may be already looking for her. Let's speed walk back." Their footsteps paced away and faded.

"They sounded like teenagers. Should we follow them?" Bishop whispered.

"No. If they caught on, we heard them it might ruin their future plans. I'll contact Officer Amato, right now. Then we'll go inside." He made the call and gave Amato the details. Hopefully, his men would arrive in time to catch them in the act.

"He said to go back to our room and wait to hear from him."

"Sounds good to me. I sure hope they find her."

They slipped back inside the ship.

She gulped the rest of her drink and set the empty flute on a tray.

Weber added his glass, and together they entered an empty elevator.

Once in the cabin, Weber stared at Bishop. "We were at the right place to hear that information and without being noticed. Too bad the other cases aren't this easy."

"Think positive. We'll get a break soon. Today was an eventful one."

"I wonder what it's like to come on a cruise and just relax and enjoy the amenities?"

"I bet it's pretty darn good. I'd love to visit these ports and see Mexico. The scenery from the ship is so tropical and I'm sure the beaches are great too. It would be a great honeymoon trip for a couple."

"That makes me laugh. Funny how that's the modus operandi for our undercover mission." He fiddled with the wedding band on his finger. He hadn't taken it off since they boarded. Bishop deserved fine wines and candlelight dinners for real. He glanced over and saw the rings on her left hand. He figured she'd worn them constantly too. Afterall it was the theme of their designated cover.

Forty five minutes later, the phone rang. "It's him," Weber said. "Officer Amato, did you find her?" He listened. "I'm glad to hear that, sir." Another hesitation. "You're welcome. It was sheer luck, actually. What will happen to those boys?" He paused again. "Very smart. We'll see you tomorrow."

"They've rescued her. She's okay and gave them the boy's names. He's already arrested them and personally locked them in the brig. A great scare tactic, giving them time to think about what they did, while he contacted their parents. The rest of their cruise is canceled, and they will deboard the ship at the next port and fly home."

"You're kidding? Their parents won't be happy."

"Understandably. It's a hard lesson learned. I only hope it cured their devious ways for the future."

SATURDAY MORNING, Bishop spread the evidence out before her on the conference table. Some of the same crew workers and security officers were involved in every one of those six missing or drowned files. She leafed through the paperwork. None of the infinite details revealed anything they hadn't seen before. They'd been cooped up all day in the tiny work room, minus the short hour lunch break. If there were a conspiracy on board, how would they figure out the puzzle? The only suspects on their list were the three security guards and several trusted upper-class crew members. Bishop kept coming to the same conclusion.

"Weber and Knight, if you have a minute, I'd like to discuss my theory about all this. I believe whoever's at fault here is running a lucrative business. They target teenage girls traveling with their families and search for those who appear most vulnerable and easier to manipulate. The group operates by carefully selecting their targets and gaining their trust over the course of the seven-day voyage. They may use a variety of tactics, from offering gifts and special privileges to creating elaborate stories designed to make the girls feel important and special. However, they choose to seduce these girls, they've made sure they turned them against their parents. In the end, they walk them off the ship willingly."

"Sounds reasonable. So maybe we should be examining the three security officers first and see what their past backgrounds contain. The salary on the ship might not suit their needs and if they are greedy, they're doing this for the extra dollars to fill their pockets," Weber added.

"I agree with checking into that. I just can't believe that Officer Amato would be involved in anything criminal. But looks and actions can be deceiving." Knight cleared his throat. "Everyone is innocent before proven guilty."

"You both have a point, but the fact remains they know we're onboard the ship posing as passengers in an effort to bring the human traffickers to justice. We need to play our roles convincingly as we sail through the Caribbean and be incredibly careful. Captain Mancini has a personal stake in this mission. His integrity and ability to run theses cruises smoothly are in question."

"They might not be the problem, but how much can they be trusted? That's the first thing we need to substantiate." Weber tossed down his pen.

"Let's check each one of the officers backgrounds with our FBI system and see what we fine." Knight tapped his computer. "I'll take Officer Rossi, Weber take Amato and Bishop, you take Ferrari."

"How about I make a twenty dollar bet the sportscar guy comes up first?" She chuckled.

"You'll win. We're not taking that bet. If it does, just keep going." Knight smiled wide.

Bishop typed the full name of Officer Ferrari into the search line and hit enter. The program brought up, *"Enzo Anselmo Giuseppe Mario Ferrari Cavaliere di Gran Croce OMRI, an Italian motor racing driver and entrepreneur, the founder of the Scuderia Ferrari Grand Prix motor racing team, and subsequently of the Ferrari automobile marque."* She'd predicted the famous racer's name would rank first on the list because of the famous Formula One scandal in his past.

She burst out laughing. "I would have won guys. No, fair. I'll try again." She entered in the full name and qualifications again. Finally, the correct bio facts surfaced. He'd attended a maritime school, took training in passenger vessel security, private vessel security, and international ship security. With his high marks, he received certification in port facility security codes, maritime law, and regulations. Plus, other specific areas like maritime safety, and the extra cruise lines requirements. Several of his credentials included certificates and licenses in basic safety courses and he met the requirements for an anti-terrorism protocol class to license him as a security officer. He had no past criminal record or arrests. Ferrari checked out one hundred percent. "Nothing here guys. His record is flawless."

"So is Amato's. It all okay. How are you coming, Knight?"

"Sorry it took me longer, Rossi is a popular Italian name. I finally located his individual files. All was good. So, that premise is off the table."

"That's correct, except now we need to obtain information on their spending habits. Do a quick credit check. See if anyone owns property or has money stashed in banks outside their regular pay range. Then we'll call it a day."

8

After dinner, Bishop strode alongside Weber and Knight, as they headed toward the Princess Theater for a famous magician's show. When it ended, her male colleagues weren't ready to call it a night.

Tired, she left them on barstools, chugging beers in the piano lounge and listening to a musician playing popular requested tunes. Her muscles still ached from that strange walking path confrontation, and she wanted a hot shower to help soothe the soreness. She rode alone in the elevator and exited on deck eight. At nine in the evening, the vacant corridor seemed eerie and quieter for a ship with three thousand passengers. Usually, the camera-secured hallways were flooded with guests. But tonight, no other cruisers joined her.

Until she heard the heavy tread of rapid footsteps behind her. The closer they neared, the more physically threatened she became. She swerved, ready to face her intruder. No one was there. Was she imagining things? She resumed her fast pace.

A door slammed shut. She jumped and spun around, again. No one in sight. Anxiousness gnawed at her insides. Her nerves were overreacting after the long exhausting day. The trauma on the walking path had left her with an uneasy feeling.

She was alone. No one had accompanied her.

They'd gotten so comfortable, both she and Weber forgot about his promise to escort her at all times. She increased her speed and soon recognized a doorway she'd passed by often with a familiar pineapple decoration. Another one had a white note-board hanging from a few magnets. The occupants had jotted messages there, so their fellow cruising friends could stay in touch. Tonight's comment read: "*Late dinner in the MDR (main dining room) and then at 9:00 p.m., let's meet up at the Disco Dance party.*" Sounded like fun if she were a normal passenger. Her journey on this ship was confidential. At this point, she had twenty numbered cabins to go and a creepy feeling haunted her every step.

She felt strangely lightheaded. Her heart pounded in her chest and adrenalin pumped through her veins. Clutching her small purse tightly against her chest, she tried concentrating on the seafoam shell patterned carpet lining the hallway beneath her feet. The designer's original nautical décor carried the same shell theme throughout the ship.

The thought brought her no comfort. Uneasy, she blamed their strict rules for stripping away the weapon she usually worn nestled into her shoulder holster. Which hadn't made her felt any safer. The Academy instructor had taught her to listen to her instincts and never panic. Her intuition had always been on the mark. She paused and took another quick glance behind her. It didn't help chase away any of her scary thoughts.

When she finally approached her cabin, she noticed a shadowy figure dressed in all black moving toward her at a quick pace from the opposite direction. She shoved in her seapass and grasped the cold metal handle, but the light remained solid red. Icicles rushed through her. Her hands shaking, she flipped the keycard and stuck it in again. It greened. She twisted the knob and pushed the door inward. The figure loomed over her.

"Mrs. Hamilton, how are you enjoying your stay?"

At the sound of her fake name, she swirled around, her heart pounding. The familiar voice resonated with her. Samson, their room steward stood next to her. Almost breathless, she said, "Everything is great. It's a wonderful cruise."

"Glad you are having an enjoyable time. I'll see you in the morning." He went on his way.

Her shoulders slumped as she slipped inside and locked the door behind her. She sighed loudly. Tossing her purse on the vanity, she saw the beds had been turned down neatly for the night. On Weber's pillow sat an elephant towel animal and the eyes were covered with Weber's sunglasses. "Wait till he sees that," she said aloud. She kicked off her heels, picked them up and glanced toward the closet.

Had someone other than Samson been in their room?

Her floor length black velvet dress sleeve dangled through the slight opening between the two closet doors. On dress your best night, she'd hung it back up neatly and pushed it all inside. She gazed around the room. Everything else looked normal.

Samson would never have left those doors propped open. He always arranged everything in the same exact way. She turned to the cabinet concealing the safe and pressed in their code. It whirred and the steel door popped open. She surveyed the contents. Everything they stored in there filled the narrowed space. She closed it using the code and stepped back.

Wait. Something look out of place.

She retyped in the code. Their gold FBI badges were on her side of the safe and Weber's passport too. That's not how they originally set them in. When they arrived, she assigned him the left side. Maybe he went in, shuffled stuff around and left it that way. Men! His desk at the administration office always looked messy. She checked their burner phones were still inside. Nothing was missing, so she locked the safe, again. When Weber returned, she might ask him. As far as her dress was concerned, she blamed herself. Maybe she'd pulled it out in haste when she grabbed her high heels before dinner.

The door flew open. Startled, she held her breath.

Weber entered and flashed a smile. "I thought you'd be showered by now." He locked it behind him.

"I'm just about ready." Should she mention her walk back alone, or would he think she's paranoid? What about the safe? She'd wait.

"Hey. Where'd that elephant come from?"

"A gift from our cabin steward. It's cute, isn't it?"

"Yeah. I heard about those towel animals. These guys work so hard on this ship, where do they find the time and talent to make them?"

"I haven't a clue." She raised her eyebrows. "Taking my shower."

"Go ahead. I'll check messages on my FBI phone."

"I'll say good night. I'm bushed."

"Good night to you." Weber plopped down on his bed. "I'll admit it, I'm tired too. But I'm not sleeping with this elephant."

THE NEXT MORNING the Beatles tune, "Hey Jude," played loudly on her cell phone about a half hour before her usual alarm. She rose, wiped sand from her groggy eyes, and snatched it from the nightstand. A familiar number flashed across the screen, her brother's nurse.

"Hi. It's Maryann, I'm sorry if I woke you. I have some sad news about Jessie."

Bishop's pulse rose, so loud she hoped Weber couldn't hear it. "What's wrong?" She held her breath waiting for an answer. Weber sat up and stared. "He's still at Mercy Hospital. Earlier this morning, he slipped and had another fall getting out of the hospital bed. He hit his head, again."

"Oh, no. How serious is it?" What could she do from here, miles from the United States and sailing in the Caribbean Sea. Good thing, she signed all those permission papers. Out of the country for a solid week, she had hoped there'd be no other problems. She thought wrong.

"They've taken him to the X-ray department. He's in queue to be screened so they can examine his skull and see if it's bleeding, again. The doctor couldn't tell me anything yet. I'll keep you advised on his condition. They were about to release him tomorrow. Now this."

"Thanks for contacting me right away. I really appreciate it. Please stay in touch and let me know the X-ray results."

"I will. Don't worry. He's in the best place he can be."

"I hope so. Thanks, again, Maryann." The call ended. She held back tears. The sad news was completely opposite of what she wanted to hear.

"Something happen to your brother?" Weber rose with a sobering look.

"He's fallen again." She bit her bottom lip. "I pray the new X-rays show no leakage of blood." She wiped a tear threatening her cheek.

"Sorry to hear that."

"Nothing I can do from here. I would like to be there for him. Except, he never knows I'm there." She hesitated. "I had high hopes, the other fall would open his mind and return his memory." She lost control and wept.

Weber went over and draped his arms around her in a tight

hug. "Everything will work out. You'll see. Before you know it, we'll be deboarding the ship and you can go to him." She snuggled into his warm embrace. His soothing words rekindled her soul, and she pressed her face against his shoulder. When he cradled her head with the back of his hand, Her heart hammered inside her, this was more than a friendship hug. When his fingers caressed her cheek, a delightful shiver ran through her. She was falling for him.

When he finally released her, his cheeks blushed a light shade of reddish pink. "Time for my shower." He went over to the closet, grabbed some clothing, and stepped into the tiny bathroom.

Had Weber hugged out of kindness, or could this be real? His compassion filled her. Something was developing fast between them. He made her feel safe and secure. And his nearness made her senses spin. She swallowed hard. Weber's last statement had summed up everything about Jessie. After this mission, they'd be back on land, and she could go to him. The doctor would make certain his health returned before he'd release him to the Brain Injury Center.

She'd never married and had no sisters. Jessie was the only family she had left in this world. All her past boyfriends were a joke. She'd chosen a dangerous job, and always thrived on a dare. She liked living on the edge. One day, she'd hoped she'd find someone like Weber, who'd appreciated her and maybe then she'd finally get married. Just now, in his arms she felt so safe, or was he only just being supportive?

∽

EARLY MORNING, Bishop, Weber, and Knight sat in the Wanderer Buffet. She spoke first. "Today's day four and we're scheduled to arrive at Roatan. During this mission, we've worked long and hard, and sometimes around the clock." She grinned. "May I make a suggestion? We need to spend more time out on the decks and even the island studying the crew and passengers. Come up for air, as they say, and observe what happens when we dock."

"Exactly, what are you proposing?" Weber bit into his toast.

"Let's position ourselves in good viewing areas and monitor who stays on and what's happens on a typical port day. Knight, I think you should get off for a couple of hours and find a place close by where you can watch the passengers and crew disembarking. Pay special attention to any crew members who reboard the ship in under an hour or so. Lots of people will come and go. Entertainment groups are known to swap ships at port stops. Another cruise ship for this same company docks here today. We already know crew members enter into a lottery system and if their number is drawn, they're allowed off the ship. Passengers and workers will be on the move. We'll need to experience the blueprint of it all and search for any signs of an abduction. It could happen right in front of us."

"Okay, Bishop. I'll take a higher deck, like the pool area with my hat and binoculars and stay on full alert. There's a miniature golf track and water slide on that level. I'll stroll around and keep a watchful eye on both sides," Weber said.

"I'll stay on the main deck and watch the crew's secret doors and people who remain on the ship. One women I met in a restroom told me all about a port day. She said the crew catches up on repair work, and while their docked they move equipment around. Plus, they wash the salt off the outside windows with a fancy system of wires and hoses. Unknowingly, those distractions could conceal something else." She hesitated and glanced around.

"An observation is quite necessary for our investigation." Knight agreed. "Most passengers can't wait to visit the countries, they'll sign up for a tour or just get off on land and shop in the exotic seaports. I've also heard repeat cruisers stayed onboard to use the Jacuzzi's and pools while the crowds are gone. Let's keep our eyes and ears open and listen in on conversations everywhere and hopefully, we'll discover something that's not right. We only have one more stop after this, and then we sail home. Most likely a person won't go missing here. I've checked the dates on all those files, it's usually the last port before sailing home. They won't abduct anyone in Miami. Too much U.S. security."

"You've convinced me, Bishop. We'll observe today. But keep you phones on in case anyone sees something noteworthy. It's settled, then. We will start this morning, after they dock the ship. We'll have at least twenty minutes to prepare before they announce the ship's gangway procedure. Knight, you'll need to change clothes and blend in with the others. Dress like a tourist, wear sunglasses and don't forget a hat."

HALF AN HOUR later the loudspeaker came alive. "Welcome to Roatan, everyone. This is Mike, your Cruise Director. The ship has been docked and passengers are now allowed to go ashore. Please find your way down to Deck One and the gangway. Be sure and bring your seapass and other photo identification with you. If you've booked a tour, the buses are parked outside waiting with the corresponding number you were given to meet your tour guide. There are several crew members standing by to help you locate them. Remember, you must return to the ship by four o'clock. We will sail a half hour later. Please stay on the ship's time. Have a wonderful day." The speakers echoed his spiel all over the ship. Conversations rose, elevators dinged, and anxious travelers filled the stairwells.

One of them was Knight.

Knight walked off the ship's gangplank right into the elevated temperatures of Roatan, Honduras. The blistering heat made him think about an indoor steam bath back in New York City. Sweat formed immediately beneath his clothing. Gazing straight ahead, he searched for a covered spot on the shore that had lots of shade and an unobstructed view of the ship. Assorted bus companies had parked in the diagonal white painted spaces on the paved dock.

Disembarking travelers were all over the place. Some stood in line for their tours, others hailed cabs, or walked the half mile into the town. Dealers for discounted sightseeing trips waited on the pier. They hounded cruise passengers and offered them lower priced tours.

Knight found empty bench beneath an enormous, tented roof that covered numerous vendors on the edge of the pier. A noisy area, he shoved in his earbuds to avoid hearing sellers voices hawking their wares to souvenir buyers. From this focal point, he took in the view of the ship's docking terminal. He'd worn his Ray-Bans with hidden camera lenses, just in case. He'd capture anyone or anything that appeared suspicious.

Knight realized this was his first observation assignment for the Miami FBI. His over six foot bulky frame made him more suited for active pursuits, but he also like giving his brain a good workout on the computer. He reminisced about his last surveillance stint in New York City.

The team watched a drug bust in a back street alleyway. Rough looking gang members with inked dragons tattooed on their muscular biceps held Glocks in their hands. They faced three other men, and one undercover FBI agent. Their extensive mission sought to remove Fentanyl pills from the city streets and capture some hardened criminals. FBI undercover officers had worked on this case for well over twelve months. The SWAT Team waited around the block as backup.

Knight and two other special agents hid on the sidelines. A sharpshooter on the SWAT Team sat atop a nearby roof with his sniper rifle aimed directly at the men. When the money and pills exchanged hands, the first gunshot rang out from above. More were fired. One gang member got nicked, but no one else was hurt. Knight entered the scene along with the other agents and kept the gang at bay until SWAT members handcuffed them. The good guys won, that time.

Today, he would observe illegally on Honduras soil, not in the good old U.S.A. He carried no gun for protection and the crime hadn't yet happened. He and his FBI team were scouting out unknown culprits, hoping to stop an invisible human trafficking ring from seizing someone sailing on the Imperium Princess of the Seas. No one backed him up. He needed to be on his game, but for who, what, or where?

He gazed at the gangway in the distance, and saw a couple walk slowly down the ramp. When the young girl stepped onto the concrete dock, the taller guy grabbed her wrist and jerked her arm. He walked briskly pulling her along. She struggled and pouted. Knight clicked a couple of photos with his Ray Bans and followed their every move. He immediately speed-dialed Weber.

"Knight, here."

"What's up?"

I'm watching a girl and an older guy who just left the ship. She's trying to pry his fingers from her arm. Come to the front section of the ship and search for a dark haired girl dressed in rosy, pink sundress. She's with a taller man wearing navy blue shorts, and a matching football jersey with the number twenty-six in yellow. He's wearing a tan ballcap, backwards.

"Okay. I see them now. I'll contact Bishop, she's on a lower deck. Follow them when they pass you without being too obvious. We'll meet on land. If we think the girl's in trouble, we can contact Officer Amato."

"Certainly. They're headed toward the vendor area now where I'm sitting. I'll listen in and see what I can find out. I won't lose sight of them."

"See you soon."

"BISHOP," Weber said. "Knight has a lead. I'm on my way off the ship"

"That was fast."

"Not sure it's anything, but he is following a young woman in a pink sundress and a male suspect wearing a tan ballcap. Meet me at the end of the gangway. It may be nothing, but we should still check it out."

"I understand. We'll take it slow. See you there."

Five minutes later, Weber spied Bishop standing on the pier. He waved and she greeted him at the end of the gangway.

"Hey, Mr. and Mrs. Hamilton. Welcome to Roatan. I hope you enjoy your day."

Weber and Bishop turned sharply when they heard their names called out. "Hi, Samson, I guess you got the day off?" Weber commented.

"Yes, I won the lottery, first time in a month." He smiled wide.

"Good for you. Have fun," Bishop said. Her phone rang. She immediately faced Weber. "It's Knight. He said the couple are shopping in that tented area and it appears their looking at hats. The man is still holding her arm tightly."

"Probably wants to conceal her face or just keep the sun off her. Time for us to shop as husband and wife, Mrs. Hamilton. Tell him we'll be there soon." She nodded.

He grabbed her hand, and they walked toward the mini shopping area. They spotted Knight, who arched a brow. "Let's go look at hats, shall we?" Weber smiled sweetly at Bishop.

Pretty soon they stood side by side with the other couple. Weber noticed the girl's arm bore black and blue marks. Bishop tried on a big, brimmed hat while Weber studied the girl in the other mirror. Could she be the same dark haired girl, Bishop had seen at their first buffet luncheon? It looked like the same guy who shoved her into that elevator. He'd worn a shirt with the ships logo. Or was it a shirt anyone could buy in the ship's mall shop? Weber couldn't be certain.

Bishop turned and whispered. "That's the girl I saw our first day. She could be trapped in his room." Weber nodded at Knight. The three of them surrounded the couple.

"I don't like any of these hats. I want to go back to the ship, right now." The girl said, and tears rolled down her cheeks.

The man's face darkened. "You're a spoiled brat." He grabbed a large floppy white hat and turned toward the counter. "We'll take this one miss." He handed her the hat and a charge card.

Weber nodded, Bishop and Knight moved in even closer.

The clerk handed him his charge card and stuck the hat in a bag.

"Miss, I sincerely want to apologize for my sister." He glanced at her. "She's autistic. I'm trying to help my mother out. She really needed a break."

"No problem. Thanks again for the sale."

Weber motioned for them to back off. They trailed the couple back to the ship and reboarded, then rode the same elevator. When the guy tugged the girl off on deck four, they exited, but headed in the other direction. Weber crept back and followed the pair to their room. Bishop and Knight waited until he returned. "What he told the clerk may be true. I'll contact

Officer Amato with the room number and verify the girl's problem. We may be back to square one."

"Figures. I need a cold drink, how about you, Bishop?" Knight asked.

"So, do I. We'll go to the buffet and meet you there, Weber."

"I need a restroom, I'll see you soon." Weber grabbed his phone and dialed.

They boarded the next elevator for Deck eleven.

ALONE, inside the in the elevator, they spoke freely. "Did you know we're on camera right now?" Knight asked her.

"No. I know they have cameras, but not in the elevators. Who told you that?" Bishop eyes searched the walls.

"The first day when you went missing, we went into the security office. We found out they have cameras watching just about everywhere on the ship. Even in here."

"You're kidding. How about in the cabins?"

"Nope. And I asked if they could listen in. They said no."

The car lowered and metal gears grounded loudly in the walls, the pulleys whined, and clanged, and then the car squealed. All of a sudden, it lurched sideways and stopped. Bishop's stomach knotted. The car remained slightly tilted, and the lights went off. She screamed as she slid into Knight.

"Oh, no. Are we stuck?" Bishop asked. Her fingers crept along the wall as she sought to stand upright in the leaning car.

"I think it's a power failure." Knight cleared his throat.

"Do cruise ships use generators for electricity? I'm really not sure how their powered." Her eyes adjusted to the darkness. Knight stood next to her in the shadows.

"I believe they have diesel-electric propulsion motors and also backup generators."

"Why aren't we moving then? There must be a call button like the hotel elevators. Maybe we can contact someone." She inched her phone from her pants pocket, turned on the flashlight and used it to locate the panel. "There's a red call button. I'll press it and see what happens."

An alarm bell rang loudly in their ears. "Yikes. That sounded as loud as a bank alarm. I hoped it alerted someone. They need to know we're stuck in here." Silence reigned for a minute. "Hold your ears, I'll try it again." She hit the button again. It rang even louder.

And then a voice echoed in the small chamber. "This is Kwame, can I help you?"

"Definitely. We're stuck in an elevator, and it looks like we're between floors, nine and ten. Can you help us?"

"Yes, hold on. I'll try to clear you from this end. It may be an electrical failure. Give me a few seconds here."

Something motor-like whirred and shook the inside walls. They didn't budge an inch.

"Sorry, Miss. That didn't work. I'll have to send a repairman. He'll be there as soon as possible."

"We were headed to floor eleven. Thank you, Kwame."

"This will take time, please bear with me. I'll keep you advised." The microphone in the tiny speaker turned off.

"We're still stuck. Why is this happening to us? I hope we weren't targeted. What do you think?"

"Not sure, Bishop. I worried about that when you first went missing on the jogging path."

"Well, the ship isn't moving yet, and passengers may still be boarding. I hope we're not stopped for a sinister reason."

"There's no one else in here. It's probably a mechanical error."

"I've never been stuck inside an elevator before, have you?" She relaxed against the back wall.

"One time in the local courthouse back in New York City. I was called to testify at an FBI hearing. We got stuck inside one for about forty-five minutes. It got hot, I remember that."

"Don't tell me that. I hope we get out of here sooner than that. I should call Weber. He'll be waiting for us."

"For sure. See if he texted you."

"I've got three texts from him. I wonder why my phone didn't alert me. I'll answer." She typed her message and hit send. The black circle revolved over and over for half a minute. Then a red message appeared, saying not sent. "Something went wrong. It didn't go through. I'll hit resend." Pretty soon, she got the same response. "Do you think the Internet's blocked in here? The text isn't going through."

"Stands to reason. This is a small space, and we're in between floors."

"Crap. Just what we need. At least I the intercom system worked."

"It's getting warm in here. I'm sitting on the floor. This could be a long wait." Knight lowered himself.

"You're right. I'll join you." She sat down and stretched out her legs. "It's sort of cooler down here."

"I wonder for how long?" Knight said.

"Good thing it's you in here with me and not Weber. He has a claustrophobia thing going on."

"You're kidding. Wasn't he stationed on a naval ship for years?"

"That's what he's said. I think the small quarters in our cabin bother Weber. I've worked with him for three years and never heard about the navy before. He's a private person and a really nice guy. Please don't let on you know about the claustrophobia."

"I won't. I've just met the two of you and so far, it's been great working here together. I really needed a change."

"This is sure a change. I never thought in a million years, I'd be stuck in an elevator on a cruise ship." She giggled nervously.

Knight laughed at her last statement.

Fifteen minutes later, she said, "We're trapped like two rats." Fear flashed through her, but she wouldn't let him know.

A drilling noise brought them both to their feet.

"Someone's working out there." Bishop sighed. "Hopefully, we'll see the light of day soon." Gears ground again and the lights returned inside their small interior. It took a minute for her eyes to adjust. "Let there be light. Now get this thing moving and open that door."

"I'll second that." Knight stared at the panel.

More technical sounds like scraping filled the air. The car shook and leveled out.

"That's a good sign." She studied the panel searching for any sign of movement or a floor number. Something zinged. They moved fast to another floor. Ten. She had originally punched in eleven. If it was working correctly, they should reach it any second.

"Deck eleven," the recorded voice stated. The doors slid apart. Passengers waited outside and stared at them, eager to board. They walked slowly off.

"Just so you know." She glanced the waiting crowd. "We were just stuck inside this elevator for the last half hour. Be sure you want to ride it." A few cruisers looked at each other, ran to the staircase and descended. Others took their chances and boarded. It was probably okay now.

She turned and caught a glimpse of someone half a corridor away, wearing a uniformed shirt watching them, intently. She tugged at Knight's shirt sleeve to tell him and when she looked back the guy had disappeared. Would she remember his face? It all happened so quickly. Maybe it was the repairman or someone checking out their exit? When she had the chance, she'd hoped to meet Kwame and thank him.

They hurried toward the Wanderer Buffet.

Weber stood there waiting at the entrance. His face wore a frenzied look. "Where have you two been? Didn't you get my texts?"

Bishop stared at Knight, and they burst out laughing. "Would you believe we were stuck inside an elevator?"

"You have to be kidding me, right?" Weber's face softened.

"Check your texts. Mine must have come through by now."

"He stared at his cell and pressed a few buttons. "Well, I'll be dammed. They just did. What the heck happened?"

"Not sure, I'm hoping it wasn't done on purpose."

9

Confusion played across Weber's face as he realized both Bishop and Knight had been stuck together inside that elevator for over a half hour. Thank goodness, it hadn't been him. His claustrophobia would have reared its ugly head. Instead, he walked the hallway and dining area over and over again searching for them. His nerves were raw. He imagined something major had happened to her and Knight. Good thing, he held back contacting Officer Amato. After a few deep breaths, he said, "Who needs a drink?"

Knight answered first. "A cold beer sounds fine right now. Especially after being ashore, earlier." He turned to Bishop.

"I'm ready. I think I'll try the blue heaven, today's drink of the day."

"It's unanimous. There's a bar right outside these doors. Follow me."

A light salty breeze danced around them as they stood at the bar ordering. They sat on the metal stools beneath the tiki hut's overhang. The blue-green waters of the Caribbean sea swirled and sent waves crashing against the white sandy shoreline. About ten seagulls lined the bank as if on guard duty.

Relief flooded Weber. He'd thought the worse and had really worried about Bishop. And there she was the whole time safe with Knight. "What actually happened on that elevator?"

The pair took turns recounting the story.

"That's the first time I ever got stuck inside one. Has it ever happened to you?" Bishop asked Weber.

"An awfully long time ago on the naval ship. And in a really small elevator. I was all alone, and it took hours to get me out. For years, I've taken the stairs and swore off riding them. In fact, this ship was the first time I ever stepped back inside one. And I'm not sure I'm pleased about boarding another one after hearing your experience." His face paled.

"It was a freak thing. No problem. I used the call button, they sent a repairman, and he finally fixed it. You can't worry about trivial things. Although, I will mention, I did see someone down the hallway studying us when we got off. He watched our exit. I noticed he wore a uniform shirt." Bishop added. "Probably a crew member making sure we came out safely. A man named Kwame answered our call. I'd like to meet him."

"I didn't see that guy in the hall." Knight chugged his beer. "But I'm more audible than visual."

"You did tell me about those cameras, so we were probably on a monitor being screened the whole time we were in there, anyway. They must have seen us on the floor."

"Weber, by the way. What did you find out about that girl we followed on shore?" Knight set down his beer.

"Officer Amato verified she's autistic, and the guy is her brother. So, that cancels that out. That next port will be the last chance for a kidnapping. We'll need to pay special attention to the crew, other passengers, and young girls. I'm not sure, but I'm hoping there isn't a leak onboard, and someone knows our true identity. Especially after your recent elevator episode."

"What about giving lie detector tests to all those in security and their upper-crust crew?" Bishop asked. "Someone could be working both sides, like the camera man?"

Weber maintained his cool when he looked at her. "First of all, we'd need a tech to administer our tests with his own equipment and here we sit miles away in another country on a cruise ship. We're not back at the Miami FBI administration office. So, I don't think that's possible. We're going on hearsay and our own theory that predetermines someone else will be abducted from the ship, even with all of their safeguards. At this point, we have to play it safe and hope the kidnapping plays out."

The loudspeakers crackled as a female voice made an announcement, "Would Hanna Parker and Juno Kent, please come to Guest Services. I repeat, we're paging Hanna Parker and Juno Kent. Please come to the Guest Services desk on deck three as soon as possible. Thank you."

"You know that that means?" Bishop asked.

"What?" Weber tapped the table waiting for her answer.

"Those two people probably haven't boarded yet. So, they are legally announcing their names to verify they're missing."

"Are you sure?" Knight said.

"I bet in ten minutes they'll make the same announcement. Mark my words." She leaned back against her chair and sipped her cocktail.

Ten minutes later, the same names came across the speakers. Pretty soon, Weber felt the ship's motor vibrating beneath his feet.

"What did I tell you guys? That poor couple are stranded in Roatan and will be finding their own way home. Happens a lot on these islands. Maybe they drank too much and lost track of time. Hopefully, they were smart enough to take their passports with them. Poor souls." Bishop shook her head.

"They're adults, so they have to face the consequences."

Knight rose. "I'm going back to the room for a shower and a nap before dinner."

"Sounds good to me." Let's call it a day. Tomorrow, we will work overtime." Bishop stood and motioned to Weber. "Okay partner, are you ready to go?"

"Sure."

"Follow me gentlemen to the elevator."

Weber's rose from his chair and trailed them. They paused and waited for him to enter first. He took a step inside the car and adrenalin ran through him. Bishop pressed deck eight. He closed his eyes for a fleeting second and hoped for the best.

Half hour later, Weber stared over at Bishop on her twin bed. Her eyes were closed, and she appeared to be asleep. Still awake, he shifted position and his mind flashed back to their morning surveillance. When he strode down that gangway plank, he peered over the top of his Ray-Bans and scanned the crowed area until he finally saw her. Sunlight shimmered a golden tint on Bishop's hair as she stood there waiting for him. Instead of fastening it in her usual ponytail, she'd allowed the curls to fall loosely on her shoulders. He admired how they framed her face and highlighted her sea-green eyes. He felt closer to her than ever before.

After she'd disappeared on the second day of their mission, he couldn't stop thinking about her. This afternoon, when she and Knight didn't meet him on deck eleven, he had another scare. Calming himself down, he told himself he could count on Knight to take diligent care of her. As his partner, Bishop exhibited bravery in awfully bad situations, but she was a complicated woman to read. He felt ready and willing for the next phase in their relationship. With every embrace the possibility of a kiss became more real. The thought stirred something in his loins. He'd find a way to make a move, but his past fear of rejection sparked in his mind. A big issue for him. Housed together in the small cabin with half a week to go, how would that work out?

A Beatle's tune played, breaking the rooms silence. Weber rose to a sitting position.

Bishop hurled her legs over the mattress edge and grabbed her phone. "Maryann. Do you have good news for me?" She glanced over at him, as she listened for a moment or two. Her facial features faded into a deep frown.

The nurse probably called with news and was updating Jessie's condition. He had hoped for the best until now.

Bishop sobbed into the phone. "Oh no. How long has he been in surgery?"

Weber straightened. He glanced at her profile, she paled. He knew the strong bond she had with her brother. The real kind that most siblings shared. This couldn't be good news. He picked up the tissue box and set it in front of her. It sounded worse than he expected. She'd need consoling after she hung up.

"Call me back the second you hear anything. Thanks, Maryann." She let the cellphone fall from her fingers onto the mattress. Her chest heaved with sobs.

"What's going on, Bishop? Is it sad news?"

She glanced at him and nodded. Her cheeks reddish and damp from her weeping. "They discovered a brain aneurysm. The doctor's operating on him trying to repair a tiny blood vessel bleeding inside Jessie's head. They're hopeful it can be controlled. If so, he'll be sedated again for a few days afterward. But there's no guarantee he'll wake up from the surgery and be normal. The best outcome depends on the patient's age and the location of the aneurysm." She blew her nose. "Age is on his side, but he could wake up paralyzed, or even mentally retarded. The diagnosis is very scary at this point."

He stood. "I'm so sorry to hear that. Especially since you were counting the days until his release. This is a real setback.

All I can say is he's in competent hands." He walked toward her with arms open wide. She stood, pressed close against his chest, and clung on to him tightly. It humbled him. She shed tears on his shoulder. Life had thrown another obstacle in her path. The terrible news really upset her.

She lifted her head and stared into his eyes. "Thank you for always coming to my rescue. I'm sorry I'm so needy, lately."

Her teary green eyes revealed the awful pain she harbored inside. He wanted to kiss her so badly. Her full lips were right below his. All he had to do was lean closer, but the timing was off. "Don't be silly. You're a strong person, and if I were in your shoes, I'd feel the same way."

"The waiting will be the hardest."

"That's true."

It would be for him too. But now was not the time to take advantage of her. He released her and she returned to the bed, grabbed more tissues, and patted her cheeks.

"Maybe if I had more family, I wouldn't worry so much. But I'm all he has."

"That's understandable. I have no one either. My older sister drowned when I was eight."

"Oh, no." She sniffled and stared at him.

"I don't talk much about my past. We all have some memories deep inside us that are unpleasant. I was much older when I found out the real reason she died. My parents finally told me the truth. Some perp drugged her, raped her, and then murdered her. He tossed her body into the river like a piece of trash." He grimaced.

"That's awful and not a good memory, is it?"

"Not at all. That's one of the reasons why I joined the FBI. And when an opening came up, I applied, and transferred into your Cybercrime, Human Trafficking and Homicide Unit."

"We were happy to have you join us. After a few weeks you

fit right in. And look where we are three years later." A quick smile flashed on her lips. "On a cruise ship in the middle of the Caribbean Sea."

"Yes, and we're trying to prevent a human trafficking abduction." He hoped she'd forgotten her brother for a moment. "I wonder what time it is?" He checked his watch. "It's already six, we should shower and dress for dinner."

"You're right. Maybe dinner and a show will help take my mind off him."

"You go in first, Bishop."

"Thank you, Weber." He sat on the couch while she gathered her things. The TV remote laid on the small round table. He clicked on the television and heard the bathroom door close behind him.

BISHOP LOCKED the door behind her and moved the towel closer. She reached in and twisted the faucet handle. The sound of the water streaming beneath the curtain soothed her. Staring into the mirror, she patted her eyes dry with another tissue. After securing a shower cap over her long hair, she slipped everything off and tested the temperature. Too hot, so she dropped it a notch, and slid behind the curtain. The pulsating warm water on her skin felt great. She let it run over her whole body to wash away the morning's sweat. She grabbed the bar soap and sponged herself. After rinsing off, she reached for her towel. Nothing like a good shower to help relax and change her mood. She needed the alone time to think. How else could she go on and accept Jessie's condition? She'd think positive and make herself believe he'd be fine.

She gazed into the mirror. When Weber hugged her this time, she felt such a magnetic tug to kiss him. Jessie's illness fresh on her mind, she refrained. How would Weber have felt about that kiss? They were getting to be exceptionally good friends, without benefits as they say. She worried, was he only supporting her because he's a well-mannered person and didn't mean anything by it? How could she tell the difference? They were there to work as a team, and she hoped they'd solve their complicated mission in the seven days allotted.

Her job at the FBI always came first in her life, not her romantic feelings. Getting involved with your partner was not an option. There were rules about that. She remembered the brief paragraph on her contract about fraternization between agents before she signed it, five years ago. If her memory stood correct, agents weren't allowed to have relations with anyone they'd worked with on a mission. End of story.

Two hours later in the main dining room, Weber took a sip of black coffee and stared at his strawberry covered cheesecake. What on earth made him order it? After prime rib, a baked potato, and soup and salad, he was filled to the gills. Tonight, the menu featured British Cuisine. The waiter insisted you ordered all your courses at once. Then he walked to a computer and submitted them to the kitchen. That's the problem right there. Whether you were hungry or not, they served it to you. He sighed and speared a piece of cake with his fork. Delicious, of course. He glanced at Bishop. She opted for a dessert of sherbet. A rounded scoop of lime, raspberry, and orange sat in a crystal glass dish alongside her. Tonight, she'd only picked at her food, Jessie's illness weighed heavy on her mind.

Conversation hummed in the main dining room and drowned out the piano music. Weber took an admirable glance around the dining area. The room was filled with assorted aged people, including children. Waiters and their assistant staff circled the tables and kept empty dishes moving. If you laid down your fork, they took your plate away and replaced it with your next course. Water glasses never stayed empty for long. Bar waiters hung in the corners and were available for ordering cocktails, wine, or champagne. The best part was the sunset around the same time every night during dinner. The large dining room windows outlined the beautiful sun surrounded by pink, orange, and yellow as it disappeared into the bluest Caribbean sea.

Out of nowhere, a man dressed in a ship uniform burst through the white crew doors of the kitchen almost knocking over a waiter carrying covered trays. Two men chased behind him. Weber saw him race from the room and onto the outer deck.

Instinct made him sprint after them. He carried no weapons. His legs and arms pumped hard beneath his dress pants and shirt. Every cell in his body was fueled by years of FBI experience. The guy raced through the casino where most people sat on stools playing slots or card games at tables. By the time he reached the area, the guy and two crew members had vanished. Weber paused and caught his breath, and someone tapped him on the shoulder. He turned. It was Knight.

"Did you see where he headed?"

"Nope. I lost him." Weber answered, his breathing labored. He leaned against a slot machine breathing heavily. "It could have been the man that kidnapped Bishop. I really wanted to catch him, so we could question him. I'll check with Officer Amato, later."

"I couldn't see his face, but the guy had a head of black wavy hair, and semi-dark skin, not as dark as mine, though." Knight smiled wide.

"That description covers a lot of the workers on this ship.

Most of these guys have thick hair, but they are younger than you and I. Some of them are a lot shorter than us. That man had a medium build and maybe was about five foot seven."

"Sounds about right."

"I meant to ask did you enjoyed that heat in Roatan?"

"Not at all. I chose a partly shaded spot under that tented roof, but the high humidity was a real killer. My last surveillance in New York City took place in forty degree weather. Had to wear a jacket over my Kevlar vest. No gloves or I wouldn't be able to fire my gun."

"By the way, where's Bishop?" Concerned, Weber stared back at the corridor.

"In the ladies room right behind us." The door opened. "There she is." Knight waved at her.

She hurried over. "Did they catch him."

"I'm not sure. They must have slipped through one of those hidden crew doors, I lost sight of them. I'll contact Amato and see what's up."

"Are we still going to the show, guys?"

"We're halfway there. I hope we can find three seats together." Weber led the way.

Sunday morning, Bishop stared out the Wanderer Buffet window sipping coffee and watching the landscape pass by in a blur. They'd sail the Caribbean Sea all day and night toward the final Mexican port and would docked in Costa Maya Monday morning. Last night's disturbance played havoc with her mind. Who was the perp racing through the packed dining room and why? Was it her abductor? She shivered. The painful memory of him tripping her on that deck resonated in her memory.

She glanced at her watch, almost nine, and their team had a

ten o'clock appointment with Officer Amato in the work room. Maybe he'd shed some light on what happened in the main dining room. She gazed at her partners empty plates. "Are you two ready?"

Weber rose. "Of course, lead the way, madam."

The team followed Bishop through the buffet exit past cruisers entering the other side. The busy area branched out like a tree in all directions to accommodate the many passengers seeking breakfast served till ten-thirty. People who slept-in had just arrived and replaced the early birds on the ship balancing out their system. The closest elevators were filled to capacity. They shuffled through the crowd to their hidden crew elevator.

Five minutes later in their makeshift office, they settled around the large wooden table. In Bishop's opinion, the windowless meeting room didn't match the grand décor of the rest of the ship. It's walls had no framed pictures or posters and were painted a dull and depressing, battleship gray. The only good thing about it was the privacy it offered. Hopefully, they'd renovate the room when they scheduled the ship for its next drydock.

Bishop turned her concentration back on the missing clues. With no leads, they couldn't predict the future. Most times when they'd investigated a crime, it already happened. The only scenario they had to go on was the chance of an abduction. They knew the endgame, but not the setup. They could only speculate on who, what and or where it would take place. So far, they found no irregular cellphone records, nothing on the crew, or any threatening messages written on social media accounts. Except for the previous case files, they had not one fact to go on.

"Knight, have you found anything new in that sixth file or on data drive? It's the only case we haven't discussed."

"I might have. If these records are current two Russian crew members were assigned on this ship four years ago. Igor Petrov and Artem Petrov. They're brothers. They room in the same cabin but were hired for separate positions. Igor's a head dining room waiter and Artem's a kitchen cook. They've never taken their leave at the same time, I find that strange."

He frowned and lines forged across his forehead as he focused on his computer screen. "Igor's human resource records show great reviews, and no past problems. The other brother, Artem, has a fine history too. Though, their salaries are not at the highest level." His fingers moved the mouse. "I've discovered a similar entry on each of their original resumes. They have a cousin living somewhere in Mexico. This is farfetched, but something triggered inside me. Instinct, I guess. So, I searched online for their cousin." He looked up and grinned. "Bingo. I found him. His name is Olaf Petrov, and I'm currently viewing his mug shot on my screen. I clicked on his profile, and it brought up his criminal records. He spent time in the Costa Maya jail for theft, drugs and assault charges. The fine printed details included his unemployment, and gang affiliation." Knight made eye contact with them.

"Interesting, Knight. Not farfetched at all. It's the best piece of the info we have yet." Weber tapped his pen on the table. "Give me that guy's name again and I'll dig in further. You and Bishop recheck the list and see if their names are listed as emergency crew workers on the back up security sheets. If they had exemplary records on board, that would be the perfect cover. We'll need to see if they were involved on every file."

"Will do," Knight answered.

A knock sounded. In walked Officer Amato. "Good morning."

They greeted him.

"Okay, team let's hear what Officer Amato has to say and then we'll get back to our work, later." Weber pointed at a chair. Officer Amato sat.

Bishop knew what he meant. He didn't want them to expose the bombshell Knight had just discovered.

"About last night. I'm embarrassed, but one of our crew members drank too much on his day off. He's involved with a woman cook, who worked beside him in the kitchen. He saw her kiss another guy yesterday. In a jealous rage, he started a fight in the kitchen. When other crew members tried to stop him, he bolted through the serving door. Two of the workers immediately followed. Eventually they caught him. He's been suspended for a couple of days and confined to his room without pay. Sorry for the inconvenience."

"Thanks for the detailed explanation. I sure hope, I didn't blow my cover when I ran as a concerned passenger."

"I believe that's the same term I told the Captain and our other employees." He smile at him. "Not to change the subject, but where are you on the investigation? We only have two and a half more sailing days before we dock in Miami."

"Nothing to report yet. It's been slow going. We're betting on tomorrow," Weber said.

"Keep me informed." Amato nodded. "I should tell you there's a wedding scheduled on board the ship tomorrow around seven p.m. Tonight's the dress rehearsal in the chapel and their pre-reception dinner will be held in the Viking Lounge on the top deck." He gazed around the room. "Weddings can cause some excitement if regular cruisers see the couple dressed in their tuxes and wedding gowns. Or the staff wheeling a large wedding cake through the hallways. People get curious. We keep them far away from where the nuptials are taking place and guarantee our couple complete privacy for their important affair."

"Understood. You and your security officers will have a full schedule," Bishop said. She studied his face and noticed black circles around his eyes. His position demanded a twenty-four hour day. When did he sleep? Most of their crew workers held two different jobs on board. Not much different from FBI employees. She'd worked crime scenes during twenty-four or even forty-eight hour stings.

"I'll bid you all an enjoyable afternoon and evening. By the way, tonight's show is my favorite comedian, I think you'll like him." He smiled at them and exited the room.

"I never heard they held weddings on a cruise ship, before. Not a bad choice and a suitable time as most cruisers go ashore. We'll certainly be busy tomorrow with all the goings on." Weber stretched his arms in the air.

"Especially if we have two Russian suspects on our hands." Bishop wondered if the wedding would complicate their investigation. Worst case scenario, if they didn't solve this problem, they'd be staying on the ship. Unwelcomed news. She'd hate to do a back2back and cruise another seven day voyage. What about her brother Jessie?

She focused on her manila files and then the monitor. Which should she start with, the paperwork or the flash drive? She opted for the computer and jotted down the men's names.

Concentrating on paragraph after paragraph of details she finally located the employees' emergency worker list. The names recorded read like the United Nations, so many different ones, and some she couldn't even pronounce. Methodically, Bishop scanned each moniker on the file's register until she spotted Petrov, Igor and then, his brother Petrov, Artem. They both were approved to help security search the ship for a woman who was never found. Officer Amato declared the woman's death an accidental drowning, that same day. Was their involvement just a coincidence? The next three file entries may confirm their findings.

~

WEBER SIGNED into the FBI special program that cataloged all the information for gangs on U.S. soil. He then searched the deportation records for gang members returned to Mexico. Ten minutes later, he stood and strolled over to the whiteboard in the corner. He grabbed a black marker, sketched a silhouette of Florida, and shaped the coastline of Mexico. He detailed the port names and circled a few well-known cartels supposedly activated in Florida. He printed the same names in the surrounding coastal towns off the Caribbean Sea.

"What are you doing, Weber?" Bishop asked.

"I'm creating a map of the known gangs and groups in Florida and their link to the cartels outside the United States. The major ones are controlled by the same families that reside here in Costa Maya, Mexico. They hire members out for protection and arrange transport of their human trafficking victims that fill their brothels and work at the drug houses. These operations are valued as a million dollar industry. They're so powerful and united, no one can infiltrate or shut them down. In our state their long arm reaches into central Florida. We've tried, but we haven't been able to stop their growth. They outsmart us every time."

"From the looks of it, we better keep trying." Bishop admired his map and considered its path to Orlando.

"I've entered Olaf Petrov's name in our gang program, it immediately returned his record with a signed, certified document stating he'd been deported. And more than once, but not in the last five years. Two years ago, the local police in Mexico arrested him and stuck him in their prison, that's why his past record showed up online. Of course, somewhere along the way, they were paid off and he was released." Weber's face sobered. "There's no telling how they get away with this stuff. It only takes one evil person inside their legal system to change sides and align with these cartel leaders. They either offer them a lot of money or threatened their family."

"It's a good thing, Knight found this additional information in the nick of time. I'm feeling more relieved about tomorrow's stakeout knowing who the suspects are. By the way, he and I just compared notes. Those Petrov brother's names were on all the emergency personnel lists. The printer is printing us each a copy of the Petrov brother's photos."

The copier hummed and whirred behind Weber's head. He swerved, reached inside the extended tray, and lifted out the six copies. He passed them each two. "They almost look like twins. We'll watch for them on the gangway tomorrow. They probably already have an unsuspecting female lined up. The App says we dock around ten. That gives them lots of time before the cruise director makes the open gangway announcement."

"They'll need the victim's seapass card and their own. It's the only way they'll be able to get her off the ship." Bishop glanced at Knight.

"They must have paid someone else to help them. After they deliver the kidnapped victim, they'll return and reboard. Someone has to cancel their victim's seapass entry in the computer system and remove her from the camera's film." Knight eased back in his chair.

"There has to be a third person in this game. Someone on the inside that's a computer whizz, who can delete pertinent information without getting caught. There's 360 cameras all over the ship." I've wondered if that same person removed my stalker's face from the video when I was abducted?"

"I'll ask Amato to check the duty schedule for that period of time. There may be a couple of men involved." Weber wrinkled his forehead.

"I'm hungry guys, anyone else ready for lunch?" Knight stood.

"Yes." Weber set down the black marker.

Soon they three agents exited the elevator and approached the Wanderer Buffet.

"Washy, Washy guys. Have a good lunch." Chanted the greeter.

"Do you think he says that in his sleep," Weber joked.

"I wondered that myself. What a boring job. He does it well. I've only seen a few wayward passengers dodge the sinks, and so far, the Norovirus has stayed put." Knight tossed his towel into a bin.

"Don't even mention that. It would cripple all of our work and we're closer than ever. Don't you think?"

"I hope you're correct, Bishop." Knight pointed and said, "I'll grab that table over there."

By the time Weber returned to the table, thick black clouds had blotted out the sun. "Looks like a storm's rolling in. We've been so lucky and haven't seen any rain." The floor dipped and rolled beneath them. Weber's face sobered. Raindrops tapped against the windows and the waves rose higher and plunged faster than an elevator without any stops.

"I'm not sure I can eat." Bishop pursed her lips

"You took those seasick pills this morning, right?" Weber searched her face.

"I did, but this ship is bouncing up, and down making my stomach churn."

"I'll get you some soup, and crackers. Don't stare outdoors at the horizon, it won't help." He headed toward the counter when the ship dipped again. He felt like he was riding a roller coaster without being strapped in. He lunged toward the serving counter and seized the edge. The ship rotated position again, a stack of clean plates next to him went crashing to the floor. He gazed back at Knight and Bishop. They stared at him while holding securely onto the table.

The loudspeakers sizzled with static and caught the diners attention. A voice rang out. "This is Captain Mancini speaking. We have sailed into a pocket of unforeseen severe weather. Hang on tight as we maneuver the ship out of the swell. It may take about thirty minutes. Access to the outer decks of the ship have been restricted due to high winds and slippery conditions, and crew member are taking all the necessary precautions to keep everyone onboard safe and as comfortable as possible. Do not go outside by the rails. The quick movements could throw you overboard. If you want to return to your cabins, use the inside corridor walls to stay upright. My men are preparing the stabilizers as we speak. They'll level off the ship. Please proceed carefully and know that my crew are here to serve you if you need additional help. I'll be back with more information when we are all clear and can sail out of this."

Weber took a fleeting chance and headed for their table. "This is so unexpected." He stared at Bishop and then Knight. Both of them appeared worried. "We better stay here, rather than try to make it to the cabin at this point. Too bad our floating hotel's really giving us a ride. Hopefully, it simmers down soon."

No one laughed at his joke.

10

Bishop held her breath as the deeper water of the Caribbean Sea rose higher and higher. Streaks of lightning and deafening thunder exploded above in the darkened sky. She flinched.

For the last twenty or so minutes, the tropical storm roiled and shifted the sea water beneath them. The downpour had worsened. Its towering waves crashed against the Wanderer Buffet's large scenic windows and the fear of drowning gnawed at her gut.

Peering through the raindrop-streaked glass, she searched for any sign of land. She saw none, only surging whitecaps slapping them on either side. Were they safe? How seaworthy had they built this ship?

"Bishop, I know what you're thinking. I'd seen this same type thunderstorm and rode many of them out in the navy. The heavy shower usually comes in fast and furious and then lingers overhead until the ship slowly sails from under it. No harm should come to us." Weber patted her arm.

Her eyes studied his face. "What about dangerous undercurrents? I heard that quick changing wave heights occur when a large set of swells rolls in and trigger a rip current. They occur when there's a break in a sandbar, then the water is funneled further out to sea."

"I don't think there's any chance of that." Weber eyes searched her face.

"I've never experienced a storm before on a cruise ship, let alone during a monsoon like this. Hurricane Andrew hit Miami in 1992, but I was only two years old. Since then, a few other storms made landfall, but passed swiftly by. So, this is one scary ride for me."

"Living in New Jersey as a kid, I've experienced a hurricane or two. But like Bishop, not during a cruise. It can't pass soon enough for me." Knight focused on the window. "Wait, is that a streak of bright light way out there."

"Looks like it could be. Thanks goodness." Bishop smiled at them both.

Ten minutes later, the sea leveled out and a steamy mist formed across the windows. The speakers hummed. "This is Captain Mancini."

A hush fell over the group.

"We're finally sailing out of the storm and it's safer to walk around inside the ship. I'm

sure, everyone's ready to resume their vacation. A word of caution, I'll need you to stay indoors until our workers have mopped all the decks rain puddles away. We don't want anyone to slip and fall. And if you're in the buffet area, please give our servers a few minutes to clean up the broken dishware before you approach the counters. Thank you all for your patience. To show you our appreciation, there'll be free glasses of champagne served in the main lobby tonight. All other indoor activities will resume in five minutes."

Cheers and loud clapping sounded as the passengers applauded. People rose and left the area. The cruise director spoke next with information about restarting the Bingo session.

"I need a restroom, before we return to our office." Bishop stood, her legs felt wobbly.

"Don't you want something to eat, first?" Weber asked.

"Nope, not at all. Go ahead you two. I'll meet you there. Please give me the key."

"I'll walk her to the elevator, Knight, and be right back."

"You really don't have to, Weber. The place is crowded." She left him standing in the middle of the buffet. In the hallway, her cell phone rang. Maryann's name appeared on her screen. She hurried toward the special elevator area for privacy and stopped inches from the door. "Maryann, how is Jessie?" She listened carefully. "I'm so glad to hear this, I can't thank you enough. Please let me know when he's moved back to your facility." She hung up. One huge problem had been resolved. He wasn't out of the woods, but on the mend."

She rode the elevator downward. No problem until the doors opened into the hallway's darkness. Had the storm knocked out a fuse? Using her phone's flashlight, she made her way to their private office and unlocked the door. Once inside, she flipped the light switch. Nothing happened. She tried it again and still stood in the dark. Making a quick decision, she stepped from the room and relocked it.

"Alpha, Alpha, Alpha, Deck Seven, Aft corridor. Alpha, Alpha, Alpha, Deck Seven, Aft Corridor." She sighed. Some crew member shouted the medical emergency code through the ship's speakers. She paced back through the darkness to the elevator and hit the button. When the two doors slid apart, her eyes squinted at the bright light. She rode to the Wanderer Buffet. Weber and Knight were right where she'd left them. She hurried in, avoiding the washy, washy guy.

"I came back. The lights are out on that deck, and our office too. I just heard the medical emergency announced. What 's wrong now?"

"We don't know yet." Weber pulled out a chair. "Sit down. I'm sure they'll say something soon."

"I'll go get something to drink, first." At the beverage area, she grabbed a glass of iced tea, and then returned to the table.

Nothing came over the loudspeaker for the next half hour.

"I suppose, we should go back to the office and see if the lights are working." Weber slipped from his chair.

The trio traveled to their office. All the lights in the corridors were back on. "They must have fixed the breaker. Thank goodness. It was eerie in here without them." Bishop entered first and they took their usual seats. "I forgot to mention, I got a call from Jessie's nurse. The doctor stopped the bleeding inside Jessie's head. He's sedated again, but only for twenty-four hours and if he remains stable, they'll keep him there for another forty-eight and then transport him to the facility."

"That's great news. I know you'll be able to rest easier now." Weber fiddled with his pen.

"I hope all goes well for him this time, Bishop." Knight lifted his laptop lid.

"I'm keeping my fingers crossed for sure. He should be in the facility by the time we arrive in Miami." She breathed a sigh of relief and opened her file. "What's the stakeout plan Weber, now that we have two suspects to follow?"

"That depends on Officer Amato, I owe him the news of our discovery. He's trustworthy and leading this investigation. I'll need his help with creating one. That's the only way this sting will work if we catch them red-handed. Don't you both agree?"

They nodded.

Bishop calculated the dangers in her thoughts. "The main problem is we don't know who their targeting. So, we'll need someone watching those men during the night on the crew's deck. Amato will have to assign a crew member who can be fully trusted. One more thing and I'm finished. What if they have access to another cabin, one we don't know about."

"Good points." Knight raised an eyebrow.

"That's why I'm contacting Officer Amato." Weber picked up his phone. Someone rapped on the door. Office Amato came in. "I was just going to call you. We've made a grim discovery."

"Before I hear your news, I need to inform you of an unplanned, dire situation. This doesn't happen quite often. We have a medical emergency onboard the ship. A male passenger, about eighty-years old slipped in a puddle outside on deck seven before Captain Mancini's last announcement. The doctor's diagnosed he had a stroke. Our medical doctors can't adequately treat this type medical condition. He'll need urgent care that can't be administered onboard our ship. Our only option is to evacuate him by helicopter to a shoreside medical facility. The Coast Guard handles this when it's a United States citizen." His eyes roved over each of them. "That means we'll have to change our course and schedule an evacuation meeting time and place, at their discretion." He paused to catch his breath. "Fortunately, our ship has a helicopter pad on the top deck. We're not sure how long this will delay our cruise. That will depend on the distance we need to travel. The Captain's arranging the meeting time now. He has to alter his charted course, and then reroute it back to the regular cruising schedule. Our docking in Costa Maya may be delayed a couple of hours tomorrow. I can't be sure."

"I understand, this has to be done." Weber nodded.

"What were you going to tell me earlier, Agent Weber."

"We've found some evidence that definitely indicates a couple of your crewmates. Researching your records and using our FBI sources, we've think two of your employees are involved in a human trafficking scheme. They have a cousin living in Costa Maya, Mexico that's a well-known gang member. He works for the local cartel. Rumors have it, the gang kidnaps women for the purpose of sex trafficking and sells them to the cartel."

Amato's eyes darkened. "Who are they?"

"Igor Petrov and Artem Petrov, two brothers from Russia."

His face blushed. "Are you sure? I've trusted those guys for a couple of years. I can't believe it." He stared at Weber.

"Their cousin's name is Olaf Petrov. The United States has deported him five times. He has a bad reputation and a long criminal record. These men may be the reason for all your problems from the missing women to the drownings. There's only one way we can be certain, and that's catching them in the act. So, we'll need your help."

"You've got it." A look of disgust rose on his face. "How'd they do this and still pretend they were loyal to me and the captain?"

"We're not sure. There's one more problem. We don't know who their planning to abduct. So, we have to keep our eyes on them at all times. Will your officers be able to handle that and the medical emergency?"

"We'll make it work, for sure. I have others that are loyal to me. This is a low blow. I still can't believe it. They're born liars." He huffed. "While we take care of our medical emergency, I'll think about how we can safeguard these men's next victim." He headed toward the door. "It's still early, but now you'll be prepared for the captain's next announcement." He exited the room.

"Who else thinks this cruise is cursed?" Bishop smiled at them both. "What else can happen?"

"Don't say that it's bad luck." Knight burst out laughing. "Only kidding."

"Luck or real, they sure have a crisis on their hands. That slip and fall is liable to bring a personal injury suit against this cruise line." Weber tossed his pen.

"That'll add to their worries, but if we fail to stop this next abduction, things will really fall apart."

WEBER AND BISHOP returned to their stateroom. They'd have supper later at the Wanderer Buffet, after they met with Amato and figured out the best way to catch those guys.

When Captain Mancini's voice spoke through the cabin's speaker box, Weber glanced at Bishop. Most passengers wouldn't be too happy when they learned about the added stop the ship would make.

When most people booked their cruise, they most likely hadn't read the fine print on the ship's ten page contract. On the last page, they just filled in the '*I did*' box and typed their electronic signature. Every passenger boarding the ship had agreed to whatever the Maritime Law status stated for their upcoming cruise. Such as missing a port due to severe weather or proceeding to the shore for a medical emergency. Lucky for them, the Imperium Princess had a built-in helipad. Instead of sailing to another dock, the vessel could travel to the nearest pickup area and allow a helicopter to land on its platform. The patient would be strapped on a stretcher and transported to the nearest hospital along with his family. The cost was outrageous, so hopefully the injured party had purchased travel insurance before they cruised. The policy coverage would reduce some of the expensive charges.

"Everyone will be advised we're sailing in a different direction. Some cruisers are bound to complain," Bishop said.

"No use worrying about it. The safety of all the passengers and crew onboard is of the upmost concern to the ship's captain.

People need to realize that, especially after the tropical thunderstorm we just sailed through." Weber gazed through their ocean-view window and saw the brightest sun and bluest skies above. The dark clouds were gone, but a medical emergency lingered on their horizon and had changed their original sailing path.

"I guess we will be meeting the helicopter and then the cruise will take on full speed and arrive late tomorrow. Not all that bad."

Bishop looked up. Her face sad, she sat there fiddling with the wedding ring on her left hand. He knew what she was thinking.

"Is Jessie on your mind?" Weber asked.

"Yes and no. He's out of danger. I just hope his body takes all this anesthesia well. That's the second surgery on his brain since the accident three years ago."

"It is, but he's so young. His prognosis will be better than most older people. He seemed to be responding well after the last operation. Jessie's getting rest and constant care. This might help him become even stronger. Who knows."

"I hope when he wakes up, he remembers me. The doctor assured me that the last surgery might do the trick. Then he had this other fall." A lone tear ran down her cheek, she swiped it away and stood.

He moved toward her, and Bishop gravitated into his arms. Staring into her watery eyes, he said, "I understand how worried you are. If you were home, it wouldn't be so bad. Except you're not. You're here, and time's not going so fast. We're working on the craziest case we've ever had. It's one for the books. Maybe someday, we can tell our grandchildren about it." They both chuckled. Her lips were oh so close, he desperately wanted to take the hurt away. He searched for the right words.

"Actually, working on this trafficking case, has taken Jessie off my mind at times." She said.

He brushed a strand of hair off her cheek and stared into her eyes. Her lashes were damp with tears. He lowered his lips, so near he felt her soft breath. His heartbeat matched hers and they kissed. Her lips were luscious, and she moved them against his. When they pulled away, he gazed at her. "I've been wanting to do that for a couple of days, now." She smiled and moved in closer. "Me, too." He kissed her deeply, again and again. The feeling was mutual.

Someone rapped loudly on the door. "It's Samson, your steward. Anyone in there?"

Their arms dropped and they parted.

"Just a minute. We're in here." He wiped at his mouth and opened the door. "Hi Samson, what do you need?"

"Are you skipping dinner tonight, Sir?"

"Yes, we are." He glanced back at Bishop. She smiled at Samson.

"I was just making my rounds and doing the nightly turn-down." His eyes searched her face and then Weber.

"No problem. You can skip us tonight." Weber shifted his stance.

"Do you need fresh towels?" Samson stood on his toes and peered into the room. The bathroom door was closed.

"Nope, we're fine for the rest of the night."

"Okay, you both have a great evening." Samson stepped backed. Weber closed the door.

"I'm sorry," she whispered, and went into the bathroom.

Not as sorry as he was. He wanted to resume what had just happened. His body was on overload. His attraction had increased in these few passing days, and he liked feeling her warmth pressed against him. He wanted to kiss her again and more. He paced the small room and finally dropped to the bed.

They worked together and they both needed to keep their focus on this case.

Fraternization wasn't allowed in the FBI or had he forgotten that part of his contract? They'd have to cool it for now. Maybe after the cruise, they could go to dinner and see where that took them. Right now, it was too dangerous to get up close and personal, especially on this cruise ship. The perps they were after were gang members, the most dangerous kind. Who knew the outcome of what might happen after tomorrow? He breathed in and out for a few moments, calming himself.

She waltzed out of the bathroom and looked passed him. "We better call Knight and develop our plan to catch these guys. It won't be easy."

"Yes, you're right. I'll dial him now."

BY THE TIME Weber reached the private office to talk briefly about their expectations regarding the sting, his nerves were edgy. He wondered if Officer Amato really believed the two men could be guilty. Bishop and Knight waited in silence while he unlocked the door. They all entered, slid into their seats, and took a closer look at the file. They'd reviewed every little detail about the Petrov brothers and their cousin from the ship's personnel files and internal FBI information. It was a lot to absorb, but now they had a good picture of things.

A key turned, Officer Amato entered.

Weber gestured at the empty chair directly across from him. Knight sat on his left, and Bishop on his right facing her laptop.

"Officer Ferrari will be along any minute. He is my most trusted second shipmate."

"That's fine. We'll wait." Weber flashed a quick smile.

When another light knock sounded, Knight rose and opened the door.

Officer Ferrari entered, greeted them, and sat next to Amato.

Weber looked around the table. "Before we start, please confirm that all conversation in this room today will be kept completely confidential in order to execute our duties, and also the plan on how to capture the person or persons in the act." Everyone raised their hands in agreement.

"Good. Let me begin. Today, we'll need to establish a surveillance plan for the next several hours. As you know our investigation of your files, and our FBI programs helped us discover that two of your crew members may be working with a human trafficking gang. For a hefty fee, these guys could be smuggling women and young children off the ship and delivering them to a well-known cartel in the Port of Costa Maya, Mexico." Weber saw Amato's eye narrow and darkened.

"First, I want to inform you that it's not unusual that sex trafficking happens at seaports.

Some survivors of human trafficking have stated that sailors can be sex sellers or buyers. In these instances, the sex buying happens at the port facilities. The U.S. Department of Justice's Human Trafficking Task Force reports that eighty-three percent of U.S. sex trafficking victims are U.S. citizens, and the average victim age exploited for commercial sex is between twelve to sixteen years old." Weber paused and drew in a long breath. "Seaports are a critical checkpoint for stopping human trafficking. Some employees, who've worked at ports in the past, have been turned into advocates for the human trafficking victims. With proper training they now know how to spot a potential trafficking situation." He looked over at Bishop. "You can take it from here."

She shifted in her chair. "To reiterate for Officer Ferrari, we have uncovered evidence that clearly indicates two crew members on this ship are involved in a human trafficking scheme. Their names are Igor Petrov, and his brother, Artem Petrov."

Officer Amato frowned, and he glanced over at Ferrari. "Neither of us have had any problems with these men on board the ship. In fact, Igor just won the employee of the month. So, it's really hard to swallow."

"We have more proof. These men have ties with their cousin, Olaf Petrov, who resides in Costa Maya, Mexico. Since Olaf is a member of a local gang and cartel here in this same city. We've also learned he served time in the Costa Maya jail."

"Bishop, please show them his photo and booking record," Knight said.

She scrolled her mouse and turned her laptop toward the officers. A black and white mug shot of Olaf Petrov and his police arrest record filled the screen.

"This is an older photo, he now has a goatee and mustache and is slightly heavier. They don't list any other names for him. When we found their cousin's name listened on each of their initial resumes, we put two and two together. It's the only real break we have on this case."

Officer Amato and Ferrari both leaned in closer. "He doesn't look familiar to me. How about you, Ferrari?"

"Nope. I've never heard or seen him. But I do know those two crew members, they both have good reputations and have been on the ship longer than me. They're always the first to sign up with security whenever we had a missing person or suspected someone falling overboard. I've worked right there alongside both of them. I've never seen them do anything illegal." Ferrari wore a puzzled look and leaned back into his seat.

"That's the problem, some people appear so innocent and then they stab you in the back. We have good reason to believe they are in league deeply with the town's cartel."

Office Ferrari stared at Agent Weber's face and said, "You've convinced me. Money talks and bullshit walks as they say. These guys don't make as much money as they liked. Maybe that's why they always signed up for the extra security duty. Plus, they're held in good standing on this ship. That makes a good reference for them if they want to move up." He sighed. "One thing worries me, though. Security workers are also privy to some of the ins and outs others don't know on the ship. Of course, we've sworn them to secrecy and even promised them a position in the future if one came available." His lips tightened. "If they're guilty. How do we go about catching them?"

Weber's face sobered. "We have to outsmart them first, by keeping each one in our sight at all times for the next thirty-six hours. I suggest we all wear earbuds to stay in touch and signal each other. You and Amato can enter the crew level without being too noticeable. Check their working schedules and off times, you'll need to keep a constant watch over them. We'll stay on the upper levels. You can signal us if they move up a deck or take an elevator." He pursed his lips. "We expect one or both will get off the ship in Costa Maya tomorrow morning, along with their next victim. Of course, I'm hoping the person won't have any idea their being abducted. These guys are so smooth, they'll convince their prey how much their into them, and offer to them an enjoyable time on the island. They'll pay for everything. So, the target is enamored with their generosity and easily lured without a struggle. Instead, they'll meet their cousin and his friends, and deliver her into their hands never to be seen again." Weber shook his head.

Bishop spoke next. "This is the only chance we have to put a stop to this gang's human trafficking scheme and arrest the Petrov's. Once they disembark, the three of us will discreetly follow them to the meetup place. We'll need you guys for backup at that point. If you have any weapons, it might be a suitable time to bring them along. They may put up a fight. After they make contact with their cousin and his friends on the pier, they'll initiate the trade. That's the moment we step in."

"Sounds like a good plan. I do have to remind you we still have that wedding. Tonight, is their dress rehearsal. We'll have to supervise that. There'll be lots of preparation going on in the kitchen for more appetizers and the actual meal. Added servers will work the rehearsal dinner. I've already checked, both of the Petrov brothers are listed on the schedules for those additional sessions," Officer Amato said. "That will keep them busy for a while."

"Good. We'll have our hands full, but it looks like this kidnapping will not be happening until the morning the ship docks in Costa Maya," Office Ferrari said.

"I agree, they have probably already selected their victim. We'll have to wait and see." Bishop clicked her mouse, cleared her monitor, and then closed the lid.

"One more point, since we really don't have authority in Mexico, I've contacted a few CIA officers, who'll help us arrest their citizens. Officer Amato as head security, you'll take control of the Petrov brothers and lock them in your ship's brig. We now have our plan in place."

Weber rose. "Everyone, please wear your earpieces on the same frequency starting around six o'clock today, until whenever we catch these criminals. I'm glad they serve coffee twenty-four hours a day on this ship, we'll really need it later. Good luck, everyone. It looks like this meeting is adjourned."

Office Amato and Ferrari stood and exited the room.

"Who's hungry and ready to hit the Wanderer Buffet?"

"I am." Bishop answered.

"Me, too." Knight chimed in. "Let's hope twenty-four hours from now, this investigation is over."

11

At precisely two minutes before six, Bishop inserted her tactical earpiece and so did Weber and Knight. Once they signed on the same frequency, they spoke to each other and made sure the audible was working. All of a sudden, two other voices joined in. Officer Amato and Ferrari. Everyone took turns communicating and they finalized their sync.

"For your information, I just spotted Igor in the dining room, he's preparing the tables for the diners, I went down one flight into the kitchen and his brother, Artem is slicing onions." Officer Ferrari's voice come through loud and clear.

"Sounds good, keep us advised. By the way, what deck is the rehearsal dinner taking place?" Knight asked.

"Deck twelve. I'm up here now," Officer Amato answered. It's getting busy."

"Thank you. We needed to know. Right, Weber?"

"Yes. I forgot to ask earlier. Okay team keep your eyes open. I'll check in with a pep talk in an hour or so, unless something happens, if so please keep me advised."

When Bishop strolled toward the buffet an elevator door chimed open alongside her. A couple of pretty blondes dressed in long strapless gowns stood chatting with two men wearing expensive navy-colored suits. They mumbled something about the wrong deck and the door closed. They had to be part of the wedding group. She smiled. Those four would experience a wonderful occasion. Unlike her. As the only undercover FBI female agent on a team, she'd be facing a dangerous situation.

Her earpiece squealed loudly in her ear. What the heck was that? She pulled it out and re-inserted it. The noise cleared. She walked into the buffet and joined Weber and Knight who were filling their plates with salad. Approaching the counter, she noticed lots of vacationers dined in there instead of the formal restaurant. She preferred to be served. Each night was themed, and she was missing Mexican Night, her favorite. She'd filled her own plate with spaghetti and meatballs and sat. Afterward, she gazed at her watch. Only six-thirty, it was going to be a long night.

The stream of diners slowed, and they closed down one side of the buffet and then the other. A waiter approached their table. He asked them to leave so the crew could wash the floors and fumigate the place. They'd been burning the midnight oil there, waiting for something to happen. It never did.

"I need some fresh air. Let's step out on the deck for a few minutes before we take the elevator," Bishop said. They followed her toward an automatic door. It's inner workings sensed their presence, and it swished open with a huge gust of air. Bishop exited into the night's darkness and smoothed her hair back into place. "Look at the stars in the sky, their shining brightly tonight."

"After that nasty storm, they better be." Knight stood close to the railing.

"It's so calm and the sounds of the Caribbean sea waves are comforting," Weber said

An engine roared above.

"Anyone else hear that?" Bishop asked. "Look over there, lights are approaching.

Do you think it's the helicopter?"

"Must be," Weber answered.

"I hear the whoop-whoop of helicopter's blades. They're here for that medical emergency patient." Knight fiddled with his earbud. "Amato, we came out on deck for a moment, and I think we see the medical evacuation team arriving."

"You're correct they're ready to land. The patient is resting comfortably on the top deck, with his family all packed and ready to board. Then Captain Mancini can turn the ship around and get us back on course." His reply filled all their earbuds.

"One more problem taken care of. Stay safe. We'll be in touch," Bishop said. The whoops became louder, and the wind increased. "We better head inside."

They took an elevator to the Shell Café on Deck five. The restaurant served coffee, iced tea and four types of pizza twenty-four hours a day, which meant they never closed. In the morning, the workers filled trays with donuts, pastries, and eggs. Or you could order a large pizza loaded with veggies like Knight and Weber did around seven a.m.

Bishop refused to eat anything and had more coffee. "Guys, we need to move to back up to the Wanderer Buffet and see how close we are to docking." They agreed and followed her into an elevator. Once out by the pool, they saw the sandy Costa Maya's coastline in the distance. Her instincts were dead on. "It shouldn't be much longer. Once we dock, I'm sure things will speed up."

"Weber are you there?" Bishop recognized Officer Amato's voice over the earpiece.

"Yes, I'm here with Knight and Bishop. What's up?"

"The Petrov brothers won the lottery. That means they both

definitely get the day off and are allowed on shore. We have to follow them both."

"Okay, let's see if there's a girl with them."

"The captain is preparing to dock in about a half hour. Then the tours are scheduled to begin. He'll announce when it's safe to disembark and where the gangway is located. We'll be ready."

"Us too. Keep your eyes on them in the meantime."

BISHOP CAME out of the bathroom changed into a touristy outfit of white capris, a flower patterned blouse and sandals. Her sunglasses and new beach hat waited on the bed. They would come in handy, later today. "You're next." She winked at Weber. She watched his eyes traveled the full length of her body and warmth flickered through her.

"You really look pretty in that outfit. I don't believe I've ever seen you dressed like that."

"I'm incognito, so I can blend in with the other cruisers." She grinned.

"That's a good reason. I'll change and be out in a minute." He closed the door behind him.

Bishop glanced at herself in the mirror. She couldn't remember the last time she dressed like this. Their jobs required a suit jacket, white blouse and skirt or pants to match. She envied women who had a normal nine to five jobs at a library or department stores, where they clocked in and out, and followed a real schedule. Would she trade this job and miss out on the excitement and weird criminal events that went on around her? She use to think not. Now she wasn't so sure.

Since Miller's death, she'd lost some of her yearning for the chase. Had this cruise restricted her or was she just missing home? If she had her choice, she'd like to be an instructor at Quantico. If they'd offered her that position, she might take it. Still employed by the FBI, but at a desk type job where she never had to leave the building and enjoyed a weekly schedule.

Weber came out of the bathroom and stepped down into the oceanview room. "Don't laugh at my hairy legs." He wore dungaree cargo shorts and a navy-blue t-shirt with the ship's name and logo.

"You look fine. When did you find the time to go shopping for that t-shirt?"

"When I returned from the buffet alone one time, they had a sales table by the pool. I've seen other men wearing them and fancied one for myself. It should help me blend in, don't you think."

"Of course, but there will be many of your twins walking around the pier. I've seen that shirt in black, too. They all advertise the ship. Not something I like to do. So many women's clothing have the designer's name etched on the back or front. I refuse to buy them and do their advertising."

"I never thought about it that way. It's a souvenir for me."

"What about the memory that come with it, working on a dangerous cruise ship?"

"I guess you can say that." He neared her. "I wish this was over and we could continue what happened the other night when Samson knocked on our door."

She remembered his warm kiss on her lips, his comforting embrace and how her body craved for more. Ignoring his comment, she smiled and shoved those strong feeling down deep inside. They had life threatening plans ahead. She'd already psyched herself up for what may happen on the pier. Too bad, her holster and gun were home in the safe. How would she survive without them? Gangs members were nasty. They'd confront them today in a strange country, one where women weren't equal. Their customs were different, and the cartels practically ran the towns. Survival was on the menu.

"Good morning. It's a beautiful day here in Costa Maya with temperatures of 29 Celsius and 85 degrees and lots of sun. No rain on the horizon." Captain Mancini's bass toned voice barreled through their room's speaker. "The tour busses have parked and are ready to receive passengers. So be sure to check in at the Princess Theater and get your group's sticker to locate the correct tour bus. The gangway on deck one is now open for passengers to disembark. I repeat deck one is now open. We will be sailing at five o'clock, prompt. Please reboard the ship by four-thirty. Tonight, Mike the cruise director will host a seventy's disco party. Check your daily compass for the time slot. Enjoy your day everyone."

"THE GANGWAY'S OPEN. It's a go, Bishop." Weber's fingers wiggled his earpiece and he spoke into it. "We're ready to deboard, Amato. Do you have eyes on those brothers?"

"Yes, they're emptyhanded right now and on the move. So don't get off the ship, until I signal."

"Will await your orders, sir."

"Bishop, I believe we should take an elevator down to floor two. Then wait for his call."

"Agreed." She shoved open the room's door, walked into the hallway and he followed.

"Are you two taking a tour today?" Samson stood in the hallway, a vacuum in his hand.

"No tour, just shopping the local vendors." Weber smiled at him. "We'll be searching for souvenirs, since it's the last port."

"Good luck. Have a fun time shopping and see you later." Samson disappeared with into the cabin next to theirs.

"Weber, it's Knight. Where are you?"

"We're headed for deck two and we'll wait by the central elevators for you."

"Okay, I'm leaving my cabin now."

Five minutes later, they met.

"This is Amato." A male voice said through their earbuds. "The subjects each have a girl on their arm. I repeat we have two victims approaching the gangway. Girl number one is with Igor, and number two is hanging on Artem. I'm walking down the last plank and I'm around six feet behind them on the pier. Our first girl has long blonde hair, braided halfway down her back and is dressed in a seafoam pants outfit, the other has dark brunette curls, and wearing a blue sundress. The brothers are not wearing uniforms. They have on navy shirts and jean shorts."

"Thanks, this is Weber. We're following but hanging back slightly."

"Ferrari, here. I'm at the end of the pier and I'm scanning the area for any sign of the

gang members. For your information, they'll have inked tattoos on their biceps with a red heart and a snake furled across it. The snake represents power and strength and the heart stands for blood."

"Amato, again. I'm closer but I don't see anyone waiting around at the end of the pier. We may have to go into town."

"We're right behind you." Weber said. "Keep walking."

Silence reigned for a few more seconds. "Bishop, here. I noticed Ferrari turned left and disappeared."

"Amato. I'm turning now. Speed up if you can. They're headed toward a bar called Sunny Taco Tavern situated near the beach. Several motorcycles are parked out front. There are some patrons at tables beneath the overhead awning." He paused. "Wait. The blonde is trying to pull away from Igor. She stopped cold when she saw the bar. The other girl is right behind her with his brother."

"Stay on them. I'll notify my CIA agents." He speed-dialed the lead man. "Daniels, it's Weber. We'll need your help. Hurry over to the Sunny Taco Tavern."

"Already here. We've been watching the gang for a half hour and trailed them. We're around the rear and plan to slip out front through the entrance."

"Sounds good, we're approaching the property from the north." Weber and his two partners sauntered along the weed-choked path tracking their targets and pretending to be tourists. He saw the bar from fifty yards away, it was weathered and in need of repainting. A large seagull sitting on the roof flew out over the water. Tourists were dining at the covered outside tables, all ignorant to the fact that a stakeout was scheduled there. There was nothing he could do to warn them.

He watched as the petite blonde girl fought Igor's strong grip on her arm. With his husky build, the guy held onto her with one hand. Four muscular gang members neared, and one pried her from him. Another man grabbed the brunette and tossed her over his shoulder as if she weighed nothing. She screamed.

Weber recognized her. The autistic girl. Why had they taken her?" He watched as a broad shouldered guy with ropy muscles, and a shaggy head of black hair wandered out of the tavern. He wore a tank top exposing his inked snake and heart tattoo on his biceps and hurried over to hug each of the Petrov brothers. Probably their cousin, Olaf. They conversed for a few minutes, laughed and he handed Artem an envelope. The gang members proceeded to drag their prey toward the tavern.

The two Petrov's got what they came for. They waved goodbye and turned toward the pier, unaware they'd been followed. Satisfaction was written on their faces. They walked straight into the path of Officer Amato and Ferrari, who'd dressed incognito for the bust and wore their straw hats tilted to cover their faces. They immediately pointed their guns at their heads. Both men stood in shock as Ferrari handcuffed them.

Weber saw four CIA agents creeping silently through Sunny Taco Tavern's front door. They flooded the scene gripping weapons and aimed at the gang members, who still hadn't noticed them. "CIA, drop your weapons, now. You're surrounded." The next few seconds, sheer madness prevailed. Gunfire blasted in front of Weber from the restaurant's shadows. Patrons at the tables darted into the adjacent area of wild Palm trees and bushes.

"Duck and cover," he yelled and sprinted closer. He had no weapon. He had no plan. He missed his Kevlar vest especially when three of gang members fired their guns. The other two struggled with the weeping, teenage girls they'd just paid for.

The CIA agents wounded two of the gang members and the rest of them raised their hands in surrender. They'd stopped them dead in their tracks. The five men reluctantly tossed their guns but two tightly held the girls in front of them as body shields. One CIA agent walked up close and confronted them. He shoved his Glock against one guys skull. "We got you. Release them immediately or I'll shoot." They both loosened their grip and shoved the girls into the agent. Then pivoted and ran.

Right into Weber, Bishop, and Knight who barricaded their exit.

Weber tripped one guy as he ran past and then landed two blows on his back. All the while, his heart thundered, and adrenalin pumped in his veins. He knocked him off his feet and when he hit the ground, Bishop jumped on his stomach. She managed to capture each of his wrists and held them so the guy couldn't strike her. The perp yelled out a few curse words in Spanish, but she kept him down.

Knight smashed into the second gang member. He punched him in the face a couple of times and held him steady until Weber slapped handcuffs on him and then Bishop's catch. They dragged the men to a standing position and led the perps toward the CIA guys, who read them their rights in Spanish and arrested them.

Bishop rushed over to the teenage girls. Both were weeping and trembling in shock. She hugged them. "It's okay, you're safe now. We're from the cruise ship and will escort you back there. It's over." The autistic girl bawled her eyes out and hollered non-stop for her brother. "You'll see him soon, I promise." Bishop told her.

Weber and Knight marched the criminals to the CIA officers. Their security had been well-planned and covered the needed perimeter. "Thank you, Daniels, and also your men." We'd never have been able to save those girls without your help."

Weber knew operating out of the country on a cruise ship would be quite hard for three weapon-less agents to put up a good fight. The CIA gathered intelligence outside of the states, but also worked hand in hand with U.S. Drug Enforcement and Mexican police. The agents would search the gang members records and if not wanted back in the U.S., the men weren't going anywhere but straight into Mexican jail.

Officer Amato and Ferrari had waited on the sidelines with their prisoners, until the three FBI agents and girls arrived. "Thank you for all your help today. Our Captain will be pleased."

They all nodded at him as if they were just cruisers who helped with the girls. It kept their cover intact for now.

Amato turned to Igor and Artem Petrov, they wore sour faces. "You two guys sure fooled me and my officers. I can't believe you were the ones responsible for all of our problems."

Igor spit at Officer Amato's face.

He wiped it off with his handkerchief. "You guys have just ruined your whole life for the mighty dollar." He wiggled the envelope in his hand. "I have nothing but disgust for you. When we get back to the ship, you're both going to the brig. You'll have one more day sailing to think about what you did and how long you'll be locked away. You'll never work on another cruise ship ever again."

THE SOLES of their shoes scraped against the pier's pavement as they shuffled toward the Imperium Princess of the Seas cruise ship along with the panic-stricken girls. Office Amato, Ferrari and their two prisoners were tens steps behind. Once they reached the gangway, Bishop let the teens climb the planks first, she followed. After each one's seapass cleared the system, the group entered the ship through the security gate. Behind them, Officer Amato and Ferrari waited with their two crewmates. They had to remove their handcuffs to get them inside.

Officer Rossi stood in the entryway reception area, along with both the girl's families. Cries of happiness, tears and hugs followed as they reunited with their loved ones. Later, they'd be individually interviewed by the ship's security officers, as would the perpetrators.

Bishop wiped a tear off her cheek and avoided the reunion. She walked straight ahead toward an elevator followed by her two partners. "Who wants to celebrate with a glass of champagne at the tiki hut bar up at the pool level?"

"Sounds like a plan," Weber answered.

"I can almost taste it," Knight joked. "And I hate champagne."

They took the elevator from deck one all the way up to the eleventh floor.

"Cheers. Can you believe we caught those guys with one full day to spare?" Bishop held her flute in the air. "Thanks to our newest partner, Knight's expertise. Without his thorough research, I'm not sure we'd solve this case. We're so glad you joined us."

"I'll second that. I hope Captain Mancini is pleased. It wasn't easy feat."

"Well, thank you guys. I'm going to enjoy working with you back on land too." Knight clinked their flutes."

"Did either of you miss your guns back there when reality surfaced, I sure did." Weber studied their faces.

"Yes. When the bullets started flying. But I've missed them all along, especially since that guy tripped me. Amato will have to find out who helped those guys inside the ship. Maybe, when he grills them, they indicate the others. That usually happens, when one goes down, they all go down."

12

On Tuesday morning inside the ships private office, the three FBI agents worked diligently with stacks of paperwork spread out on the table. Above them the air conditioner hummed, and their half empty coffee mugs sat beside them. As the last full sea day on the seven day voyage, they had no other choice but to finish their reports. Tomorrow they would disembark.

Weber fingers typed in the keyboard inputting his data for the final covert mission report required by the bureau. He listed his classified intel and experiences leading up to solving the cruise lines sabotage. "This whole situation was quite an ordeal. Now I'm finding explaining it on paper is even tougher. I keep merging the stages and recording the hours alongside them, and then I have to go back and include stuff I've somehow forgotten."

"Me, too. It's complicated and not like any other case we had to report. You know the Director wants all the details logged in there for every step of the way. That's hard to determine with all the other happenings around here. Are you mentioning my kidnapping?"

"I did," Knight said. It's supposed to be listed, right."

"Of course, it adds more working hours for us. Similar to blowing your cover and being caught by the bad guys when your stakeout goes awry. Our jobs are full of twists and turns and unplanned events. A doesn't always lead to B, and so on. You follow me?"

Weber glanced over at her and said, "You can say that again." They all laughed.

"Big question, do you think a reporter will get hold of this story?" Bishop asked.

"If they do, they can't have any knowledge of FBI working the case. Remember its confidential all the way on both sides." Weber answered.

"That's true. Think about the bad publicity it would cause for this ship when the blame's on their actual crew members. It's like admitting their own guilt. They'd be liable and I think they'll want this story buried."

"Good point, Bishop." Weber returned to his monitor.

They all quieted down. Until someone knocked on the door.

In walked Captain Mancini and Officer Amato.

"Good morning, everyone. I had to come down here when Officer Amato told me the good news. I want to shake all of your hands. He filled me in on the real reason for our ships past difficulties. I was horrified to learn that some of our crew members were the cause. So be it." He circled the table and shook their hands.

Amato followed him around and shook them a second time.

"It looks like you're busy, so I won't keep you. Thank you all again." Captain Mancini exited the room.

"Do you have a few minutes to spare?" Amato asked. "I have answers to a few questions you'll want to hear."

Weber lowered his laptop lid. "We're all ears."

"When we got back yesterday, I interrogated each of the brothers for about two and a half hours. I had them in separate rooms of course. The younger one, Artem finally broke. He told me they'd partnered with an employee onboard who had excellent computer skills. I called him a black hat. He didn't know what that meant. Bishop, I remembered you mentioned a well-experienced computer tech could slice frames from film and delete a seapass from our system. That was right on target. I just arrested Officer Rossi."

"Whoa." Bishop said. "He's one of your finest officers. But I don't understand, when we reboarded, he greeted us and the girls with their families."

"Yes. Unfortunately. When I interrogated him, he confessed immediately. I stuck him in the brig too."

"I have a question to ask you. Did he own up to removing the man's face who attacked me from the actual film he showed you? Or didn't you ask him?"

Amato's face filled with sorrow. "Rossi admitted he'd changed the film before we even went in there to find you. I'm so sorry that happened."

"By the way, who actually attacked me?"

"Another well-trusted person and a floor manager on this ship." He hesitated, Samson, your cabin steward.

She gasped. No wonder his voice sounded so familiar.

"He was involved with the Petrov brothers and knew all about their operation. They paid him to tell them when attractive teenage girls checked into a cabin on his floor."

"So why did he kidnap and drug me?"

"When I questioned him, Samson said that first day he delivered the bottled water to your room, he noticed the safe door slightly ajar and a gold badge sparkled at him. Curious, he pulled it out and read your FBI ID status. He immediately bragged about it to the Petrov brothers. Worried, they offered him a good sum of money if he drugged you and threw you overboard. He agreed. They gave him the drug, probably stolen from our infirmary."

Bishop flinched.

"When it came time to actually do it. His conscience stopped him. So, he stuck you in that bathroom instead. He gave back their money and made excuses. He told them you were here on your honeymoon, and he'd keep his eye on you. He worked hard to convinced them you weren't a threat. They believed him. And in the end, he avoided a murder charge. Although, I had to fire him. The jail now holds four of our own crew members."

"I remember when we first arrived, I put all my stuff inside the safe and told Weber the code. We left the room for the sail away party. When we returned, he mentioned it was unlocked and he hadn't put anything inside yet."

"For your information, as a floor manager, Samson could have opened your safe any time he wanted too. He has a special key."

"I think he did, a couple of days, later. Things were shuffled around in there. I wondered why? Plus, he kept showing up at all different times. We ran into him on the shore and many other places. So, he did keep his eye on me."

BISHOP STOOD next to the twin bed and unzipped her suitcase. Lifting her new bathing suit and coverup from the vanity drawer, she'd noticed the store tags still attached. "I guess we didn't need a lot of this stuff we bought for the trip." Folding them neatly, she packed them in her bag.

Weber stood aside her with his suitcase flapped open. "Time went so fast, and we were so involved in this investigation, we hardly had time to come up for air. I wished I had time to put on my bathing suit and soak in those hot tubs. They looked so inviting, especially after our long days in that private makeshift office. I'm not complaining, but the cruise went better than I expected. It's hard to believe it's over already."

"If we hadn't found that cousin, we'd be stuck here for another seven days. I'm ready to get back on dry land see how my brother made out, aren't you?"

"Yes and no. I'll sure miss that Wanderer Buffet and the main dining room. I don't cook much and probably gained a few pounds." He turned toward her, in the small room. "You know what I'll miss the most."

"What?" She turned and stared into his hazel-green eyes.

"You." A small flicker of a smile rose on his lips. "You've grown on me. Listen, Bishop, I think I'm falling in love with you."

Her lower lip quivered. The sight of his clean-shaven face and neatly combed hair made warmth rush through her. Realization dawned. She cared for him too. "We both work a dangerous job and neither of us can be certain of tomorrow."

He pulled her against him. They hugged. "That's why we need to live for today. I'm tired of being alone. We're a surprisingly good team at work and we respect each other." He leaned down and kissed her. Their lips parted and he said, "You feel something, don't you?"

Dazed, she let the words sink in. "Yes, I think I'm in love with you too." His eyes met hers and the heat from his body comforted her. They'd only been together a handful of days, yet she felt sure of her heart.

He caressed her cheek. "You need to know what you are getting into."

"I already do, you don't have a house and you need somewhere to live." She chuckled. "Not really." She melted against him. He wasn't joking.

"We can sell yours and buy one together if that would make you happy."

She moved away and said, "Let's get this packing done, dress up and celebrate our last night as a normal couple in the main dining room. They don't want the suitcases outside our door till after ten p.m."

THE NEXT MORNING, Weber and Bishop gathered their toiletries and made sure the closet, drawers and safe were completely empty. Grabbing their carryons they exited the cabin for the last time. They'd been assigned to wait in the Princess Theater along with Knight until their deck number was called. Weber thought about boarding day. All the passengers were ecstatic when they climbed on board, but now most of the cruisers were frowning about going back to their normal lives.

And them theirs. He immediately thought about their emergency situation. He didn't say a word to Bishop, but quickly texted the FBI personnel department. They assured him a couple of men were already scheduled to greet them at Miami's pier. It seemed like they'd left town ages ago. Would eight days be long enough for those gang members to stop searching for them? He thought not.

When they finally called their number over the loudspeaker system, they hiked behind the crowd to the warehouse that housed all the luggage. After locating their suitcases, they rolled them toward the uniformed security officer standing at the custom podium. Once there with passports in their hand, they passed through and were escorted outside into the sultry Miami heat pickup area. They walked slowly to the parking garage. He wiped his forehead and loaded their belongings into the trunk.

They both got in. Weber fastened his seatbelt and stared through the front window of his Suburban.

"Someone's cracked our windshield."

Bishops looked up. "You're kidding. I thought this parking area was protected."

"So, did I. Let's get out of here. The rookies are supposed to be out there waiting to follow us home." He drove out the signed exit behind other vehicles and then turned onto the main highway. "Maybe we should stop at the administrative building first, before driving to your house and find out where Miller's case stands. I'll have to drop this SUV off at the FBI garage anyway, we can't drive it with a broken windshield. I'll exchange it for yours, they must have installed the new tires by now."

"Weber, I've been thinking. If there's an opening at the Quantico Academy for an instructor, I'd like to apply. Would you be willing to transfer to the Virginia area and work at the Norfolk administration building? They are only thirty five miles apart. We could buy a home somewhere in the middle and I can move Jessie to another facility. It could all work out."

"Yes. How did you come up with that plan so fast? I think it would a perfect way for us to stay safe." He zoomed through the next green light. He hadn't thought that far along.

"I thought about Santiago. I'm sure he had Miller killed and he won't stop chasing us. Our case on Miller is back at ground zero. I'm afraid for our lives after what happened before the cruise and now after. She pointed at the windshield. The Director would probably agree, even if he put us in a safehouse, they'll find us before long. Knight will need a new partner or two and there are some rookies close to promotion that should be able to take over our division. They can always contact us with questions. We're really in need of a fresh start."

"That's a good idea, Bishop." His glanced over at her at the next red light. "Can I call you Elaine and you call me, Mike?"

"That's going to take some getting use too. But why not."

"I'd really like to call you, Mrs. Elaine Weber if you'll have me?

"Are you asking me to marry you, Weber?"

"It's Mike and yes. What's do you say?"

"I'd be happy too." Her face blushed. "If you promise to take me on a seven day non-working cruise for our honeymoon."

"Considerate it done." The light greened, and he drove with a smile on his face.

"Hey Jude" played in the interior of the van. Bishop answered. "Maryann, we're back in town and on our way to the hospital. How's Jessie doing?"

"He's not at the hospital, Bishop."

"What happened now?" Her eyes narrowed and she looked at Weber.

"Stay calm, your brother's right here at the Brain Injury Center, and he want to say hello."

Made in United States
Orlando, FL
13 August 2023